August Heat

A Year in Paradise #8

Hildred Billings
BARACHOU PRESS

August Heat

Copyright: Hildred Billings
Published: 10th August 2019
Publisher: Barachou Press

This is a work of fiction. Any and all similarities to any characters, settings, or situations are purely coincidental.

Chapter 1

KRYS

The smoldering remains of the Longfellows' barn was not the prettiest sight to the behold. Only the oncoming gray clouds gave any hope that the worst of it was over, since two hours' worth of dousing had barely been enough to put out the flames.

"Never gets any easier," Sean Quimby said. He sat in the dry earth that would soon glisten with freshly fallen rains. Beside him, Krys Madison removed her helmet and ran her hand through her flattened hair. Sweat gleamed on her brow and tickled her skin beneath her uniform. Nothing like fighting a raging fire on a day already thick with humidity. "At least it's over."

"For us, anyway." Only a few yards away stood Ethan Longfellow, one hand on his pale face and the other clutching his cell phone. He lamented that he didn't have decent reception that far away from his house, but he didn't have the heart to call his wife and tell her what had happened to the barn. "The Longfellows are gonna have fun with their insurance."

"At least there was nothing living in the barn." Ethan shrugged. "Aside from some rats, maybe. Ugh. Great. Now I'm gonna think of cooked rats. I'm gonna figure out when we're good to go so we can get outta here and have a shower."

"You do that." Krys was too tired to get up. She had been up half the night tossing and turning, thanks to her oscillating fan dying a grand death in the middle of summer. While that season had been milder than recent years, the humidity had been killing Krys, who wasn't used to wet, moist summers. Some of her fellow firefighters came from the east coast, be it New

England or the South, and they loved to pick on the locals for succumbing to the sweats more easily than most. *Never mind a damn tornado touching down in Portland last month.* Hail wasn't supposed to mean anything more than some rain in those parts. Yet when the Midwestern transplants began to shake in their sandals and ran for the nearest cellar (only to discover a *lack* of cellars in Paradise Valley) Krys finally got her turn to laugh.

She wasn't laughing much today.

Between the lack of sleep and crushing sense of futility, Krys had been battling the kind of seasonal depression that didn't often affect those in the northwest. While everyone else turned on their specialty lights in the winter, Krys shuttered up her windows in the summer and pretended the sun wasn't up until 8:30 PM most of the season. She blamed her PNW nature that discredited the sun as a fabrication of the cosmic mind. No, she wasn't sickly pale and lacking in Vitamin D. If anything, she tanned too easily. Krys's problem wasn't about the *weather,* necessarily... although the dry heat and droughts that had plagued the northwest for the past few years certainly didn't make her job easier.

She hated how *happy* it made everyone.

All right, so I hate seeing that long face more. That was the hardest part of this job. Approaching property owners and giving them the bad news. *"Sorry, Mr. Longfellow. We couldn't save your house, your barn, or your family."* So, it hadn't been that bad this time. The barn hadn't been used for years and had fallen into disrepair. Still, it was a massive cleanup the Longfellows would have to pay for, and if Ethan hadn't happened to be driving by when the fire began to rage, it could have spread to the nearby woods or the family house. No, the worst was the house fires that completely obliterated a whole family's life. Even if nobody died, it was like something had. *A few months ago two little girls lost the only home they ever knew.* Krys had gone back after that housefire to help them scavenge for anything that might still be salvageable, knowing how fruitless it often was. What wasn't charred was ruined by smoke damage. Still, when a six-year-old cried about the stuffed bunny that had helped her survive life so far, Krys was inclined to follow the sounds of her heartstrings and do what she could. Sometimes that meant digging into her own toy closet back in her parents' house in Portland and unearthing a few stuffed animals she no longer needed. She figured it was better than touring little kids around thrift stores.

"Madison!" called the chief. "You done sitting on your ass yet? I need you to do a sweep of the area."

She raised her hand in acknowledgment, but was in no hurry to leap up and get back to work. If anything, her legs were sorer than ever, and the depressing need to go to sleep seeped into her bones.

That was probably why the chief put her on sweep. All she had to do was look for anything out of place, embers in need of quashing, and creatures requiring aid. Most of her coworkers were already sifting through the debris of the barn in case someone *had* been in there. The most likely starts of abandoned barn fires were high school kids smoking and getting up to no good. But that was for the fire marshal to figure out when he got there. Krys was simply grateful it was toward the end of her shift. With any luck, she'd be in bed within three hours.

Luck was not on her side that day. It was on someone else's.

Or should I say someones... At first, Krys hadn't heard the pathetic mewling coming from the tall grass by the woods. She was so focused on her own problems and crappy feelings that she almost stepped on the box of kittens halfway through her sweep.

"What the..." Her foot had kicked aside the box. Four fuzzy heads jerked to left, mouths opening and cries of helplessness stabbing Krys right in the heart. "You've gotta be kidding me. Who the hell left a box of kittens here?"

Seriously. Kittens.

Now, Krys was a dog person, not that it meant she purposely went around kicking boxes of kittens for fun and slander, but she knew way more about puppies and dogs than she did about kittens. She couldn't gauge how old they were. All she knew was that there were four, with no mama cat in sight.

"Here, kitty kitty." She looked around, including in the tall grass and a few steps into the woods. Between the sounds of birds kicking up a fuss in the trees and her fellow firefighters shouting things to one another in the distance, Krys couldn't hear the potential cries of an injured mama cat. *Don't tell me these fuzzballs were dumped.* Unfortunately, that was common out in those parts. Farmers and ranchers would bundle up barn kittens they ·didn't want and take them elsewhere, sometimes way too early. These kittens looked barely weaned, if at all. They were big enough to hop out of their box, but either fear or a lack of energy kept them contained.

Well, there was only one thing for Krys to do.

She removed her jacket and draped it over the box, careful to leave a big enough hole for air. Gingerly, she picked up the box and carried it back toward the burn site, where Ethan Longfellow spoke with the fire chief.

"Excuse me, Mr. Longfellow," Krys interrupted, when there was a brief lull in their conversation. "I found this box of kittens a few yards away from here, toward the woods. Do you know anything about them?" *Please tell me they're yours. Please tell me they're your barn cats that magically escaped with their lives.* This would make things so much easier. Boom. Congrats, Mr. Longfellow, you have a smoldering barn on your hands, but the kittens survived! It's the miracle of life! (Honestly, it was a better outcome than most barn fires. Krys had a tough stomach, but still had the occasional flashback to what poor animal was found in the cinders.)

He blankly looked between her and the kittens crying in their box. One particularly fluffy cat had climbed on its sibling and attempted to poke its head out of the box. All that happened was them both crumbling to the bottom.

"I've never seen them before in my life," Ethan said.

Great.

"You found them in a box like that?" the chief asked.

"Yup. Right over yonder."

Both the chief and Ethan looked in the direction Krys pointed. When they put the focus back on Ethan, he shrugged and said, "No idea about it. They're not my cats. Glad they weren't in the fire, though."

The chief shrugged. "Get 'em to the shelter."

That was the proper course around there, but Krys also knew how overcrowded the county shelter was. While kittens were more likely to be adopted than grown cats, the odds still weren't great. *You know, I may not be a cat person, but I'm not sure I'm comfortable taking them to more of the same.*

Ethan stopped her before she turned away. "There's the vet, you know. I hear she takes in some of the smaller critters sometimes, especially if they're really young or hurt. Nice lady. She helped us when our chickens were going crazy."

"What vet?" Did he mean Dr. Global in town? His clinic was the closest thing to an animal hospital in their corner of the county, but Krys didn't know much about him, other than the clinic was tiny and some people in town complained that he took the easy way out of diagnoses. Most pet owners drove a few extra miles to the county seat for a "proper" vet clinic.

"You know, the farm vet." Ethan looked at her as if she were nuts. "I mean, don't she live in town? I know I see here there all the time. Dr. O'Connor!"

"O... connor?" Krys didn't know anyone with that last name. *Here I thought I knew as many people as the mayor did.* Came with the territory of fighting fires. If you weren't putting out everyone's messes every other week, you were entertaining their kids at school.

"Yeah, yeah. Sigh-o-vaughn or something."

"Sighovaughn O'Connor?" That wasn't a real name. No way.

"Know what? Think I got her card here in my wallet." Ethan looked plenty appreciative to have something take his mind off the death of his old barn. He fished out that wallet like he was about to give Krys some candy.

The card was soon between her fingers, although her arms continued to prop up the box of kittens. One of them had taken to rubbing its face against her hand. Poor buddy must have been cold and scared. *Damn poor, scared animals.* Didn't matter if Krys were a cat person or not. She saw a scared, helpless baby animal? She did something about it. The guys at the firehouse would give her crap, but deep down they were all softies, too. Took a big ol' softie to do a job like theirs.

"*Siobhan O'Connor – Agricultural Veterinarian.*"

"She look as Irish as this name sounds?" Krys asked Ethan.

"Is that what it is? No wonder I can't say her name. It's all Greek to me."

More like Gaelic. "I'll try her. Thanks."

She took the box of kittens back to the truck, where she kicked open a door and shoved the box onto the seat. After reclaiming her jacket and making sure the kittens wouldn't fall from any untimely heights, she slammed the door shut and approached Quimby by the cinders.

"I've got cats, man," she told him.

"Cats?" Quimby whipped his head toward her. "So, we're jumping over the P word now and going straight to cats, huh?"

"Not like that, you dumb perv." Krys had heard every lesbian joke under the sun, having lived in Paradise Valley, but nothing compared to working with a bunch of grown men who spent too much time staring at naked-lady posters and pitching in to get Cinemax for the station TV. They were polite to every lesbian in town. Except Krys. Because she was one of them, which meant she was up for ribbing about anything and everything. The fact she *looked* like them probably didn't help her case. "I mean actual cats. Found a bunch of kittens in a box over by the woods. Longfellow says he doesn't know anything about them, so I'm taking them to a vet as soon as we get out of here."

"You mean Dr. Global? Not sure how much help he's gonna be. I took a stray dog in once to look for a microchip, and he acted like he never heard of the damn things."

"No, some other animal doc. Here, he gave me a card." She passed it to Quimby, who looked it over with mild interest. "You ever heard of her before?"

"No clue. But if she's half as cute as her name, you should hook me up, yeah? Assuming you're not gonna make your move before I do, Madison."

"Very funny." The ribbing came from a real place, after all. Until that year, Krys had been an unapologetic womanizer who knew every woman in town. *That means I* know *most of them*. Even if her carnal knowledge was not complete, she knew some pretty juicy drama. This was a woman who had always slept with her friends. More like she slept with them first, *then* they became friends... and those friends ran off with celebrities...

"You know I just josh you."

Krys decided that was a good time to check on the kittens again. How long until she figured out who this Dr. O'Connor was?

How long until the distraction was over, and she returned to her seasonal mope-fest?

Chapter 2

SIOBHAN

"That's a pretty determined girl right there." The porch creaked beneath Siobhan's weight as she leaned forward and brushed her fingers against the cat's arching back. Giant pads for paws swatted at her before the cat scampered away. "She must have a giant will to live."

"You think so?" asked Rita Mills, the lucky new owner of the cat pouncing on a bug.

"Animals are a lot like people in many ways. Some have a greater will to live than others. Not every cat who gets hit by a car like that one is gonna bounce back. You can take two cats of the same physical health, hurt them in the same stupid way, and one will live while the other dies. Like people."

"Huh. Never thought of it that way." Rita gazed at the gray American shorthair with new appreciation. "I was gonna name her Angel, you know, 'cause it's like she had a guardian angel watching over her, but now maybe I'll name her after my grandma who lived to be one hundred despite all her health problems. Real spiteful one, that lady was."

Siobhan chuckled. "Careful that you're not summoning your grandmother's spirit in that cat. She might have been sent to spy on you."

"Oh, now don't go putting that crazy stuff in my head! I'll totally believe it!"

The cat raced back with a trill in her throat. Rita gave her a light pat to the rump while Siobhan took another look at the twisted tail crinkling up into the air. The poor baby had been hit and ran over in such a way that she would have lifelong hip problems and lose half her tail, as soon as it got around to falling off. But she seemed to be in good spirits and better shape than most cats like her would be. *Like I said to Rita, it's a will to live.* This cat had bugs to catch and sun to sleep in. Sooner or later she'd succumb to the end like every living creature, but with any luck, she'd enjoy a nice, full life first, because there was no way she was any older than a few months right now. *Her growth will be stunted because of her injury, and she has extra toes, which means she's probably inbred somewhere in her recent genetics. Good golly, maybe the cat is too stupid to realize she shouldn't have made a full recovery.* She certainly would look goofy once she fully grew into forced-munchkin status and lost half her tail. Siobhan hoped for plenty of photo updates. Hell, was this an awkward time to suggest Rita learn how to use Instagram and get to photo-taking?

Siobhan didn't treat a lot of house pets in her career as a big animal vet, but there were more than a few rural pet owners who couldn't afford to drop everything and take Fluffy to the only vet clinic for thirty miles. So they called Siobhan, who dropped by whenever she had a chance. In the case of surgery, though, she referred them to an animal hospital on the coast. *Not like I can perform surgery right there in their living room, anyway.* It was easier for her to charge a little extra for a house call than to convince some people to take their pregnant dog to the vet to make sure everything was in order. Besides, if she had the time, dropping by to say, "Yes, take the dog to the damn clinic," at no charge usually got people moving.

Cases like Rita's cat, though, were exactly what she made time for in her busy schedule of hopping from farm to farm to check on livestock. She occasionally got a call to help a sick or injured wild animal as well. The bigger, the better! *Never forget the time I looked an elk right in the eye and saved his leg, and therefore his life.* Rita, on the other hand, had called her two weeks ago bawling that she had found this poor, injured cat in the middle of the road. "Thought it was dead first, so I kept on driving," she said between sobs. "Then I look in the mirror and she pokes her little head up like she's saying help me! I had to turn around and now I've got this cat on my porch that I don't know is gonna make it. You gotta come at least look at her, doc!"

After a thorough exam that determined no surgeries were probably necessary, Siobhan prescribed some antibiotics and wrapped the crinkled tail in a bandage. She came back today to check in on the kitten and was pleased to see her bounding across the couch and beseeching attention around every turn.

"She's very lucky you drove by that day," Siobhan said to Rita. "Too bad we can't figure out who put her in that position to begin with, but she should be fine. It all works out in the end."

"A thousand years of bad karma to whoever dumped her there, anyway," Rita spat. "Who the hell dumps pets? There's a damned shelter not too far away from here. Why are people..."

"One of many human mysteries." Siobhan stood up and shook Rita's hand. "Give me a call if anything comes up with your new addition. I'll check in from time to time."

Siobhan hopped in her truck and checked her phone for any messages. The only thing of note was a garbled voicemail from her assistant back at the office. *AKA my aunt Gabriella.* They shared a house off the county road that conveniently doubled as a vet office. Nothing fancy, of course, but it gave Siobhan a place to treat the occasional animal and to safely store her equipment. Sometimes that was a bigger boon than renting out a space in town. Kept out the nosy people that way.

Besides, Siobhan liked being by herself. She preferred life away from the hustle and bustle of a town, even a small one like Paradise Valley. *To think, I moved here to be closer to people "like me."* It hadn't been her idea, but she went along with it because her ex insisted it was the place for them to make their "homesteading dreams come true." Siobhan needed a new place to practice and discovered there was an opening for a livestock vet more local to the area. It had seemed like destiny at the time.

You may notice a lack of a partner in this house, though. Her aunt didn't count. Gabriella picked up the pieces Emily the ex left behind. Namely, she came to make sure Siobhan didn't die from the breakup. She stayed because she loved the area and the isolationist lifestyle it provided.

Siobhan shut off the engine as soon as she parked in her usual spot, right between the house and the RV garage she converted into her office space. She wouldn't head into the house yet, though. First thing? Into the office, where she'd fill out some paperwork about Rita and anything else she did that day. Luckily, she currently had no wounded or sick animals staying for treatment in the back of the office. Otherwise, she'd spend the rest of her evening there.

"Oh, there you are!" Gabriella popped out of the office, her windbreaker freshly put on and her hair up in a messy bun. "Been trying to get a hold of you. Did you get my voicemail?"

"Not really. I got it, but it's not super understandable."

"Dangit. You've got somebody coming by with some kittens soon."

"Kittens?"

"I guess that old barn on the side of the route burned down or something. One of the firefighters called earlier, saying they found a box of kittens nearby. Owner of the barn says they aren't his and suggested the firefighters bring them over here."

Siobhan slammed her hands on her hips, a worried look gracing her freckled visage. "Kittens? Isn't that more suited for Dr. Global?"

Her aunt shrugged. "She's coming by soon."

"She?"

"Yeah, it was a female firefighter who called. Is that weird or something?"

"No." Siobhan pushed past her aunt and entered the office. "Not weird at all."

She didn't want Gabriella seeing the dread on her face. Although Siobhan didn't personally know Krys Madison, she *knew* who she was. *The only female firefighter in Paradise Valley. Kind of a big deal.* Krys had many, many acquaintances. When she wasn't at the firehouse, she hung out at the gay bar or got into trouble with her friends. One of those was her ex-girlfriend Jalen Stonehill, a plumber who came by the O'Connors' to take care of their ongoing issues. Jalen hadn't been around too much lately, though. She was too busy living it up in Hollywood with that new celebrity girlfriend of hers.

Sheesh. Siobhan made a point of avoiding town gossip, yet she still knew all about *that*.

Like how she also knew that Krys was the kind of trouble Siobhan didn't need in her life.

A car pulled down the driveway a few minutes later. Siobhan had barely begun her paperwork when she caught sight of a muscular woman popping out of the car and turning around to pick up a box from the backseat.

Here we go.

Chapter 3

KRYS

"Hello?" Krys looked between the old house at the end of the driveway and the big garage beside her. The garage was marked *Clinic,* but it didn't look like anyone was inside. So much for being prepared and picking up the kittens while she thought about it. Maybe she should put them back in the car, in case...

A door popped open beside her. "You must be Krys. Madison, right?"

Krys whipped around, jostling the poor kittens in their box. Mews of displeasure peppered the muggy air.

Yet Krys didn't have much sympathy for the kittens who had already accomplished such a big day. She was too taken aback by the woman standing in the doorway to her clinical office, arms crossed and demeanor bold enough to start a few fires. *Guess I'm the one to do that around...* Krys knew something about putting out fires.

She also knew about stoking them.

The woman in front of her couldn't have been much older than thirty-five, possibly younger. Not exactly the picture Krys had summoned when she heard about a rural vet with an older, more traditional name. Yet she wasn't that far from her picture of someone named *Siobhan O'Connor.* She may have lacked some age, but she had orange-red hair that was the color of flickering flames before they turned into raging fires. Freckles that were as plentiful as they were emboldened with a golden-brown hue dotted her pointed face. Such a self-assured attitude cocked against the doorway, a flowy white top hanging loosely from a willowy frame. Black yoga pants added an air of countryside authority before Krys got a load of the dirty, old, *worn* work boots scraping against the ground. *Those things look like they've walked through a few cowpies.*

It didn't detract from Siobhan's beauty, though. If anything, it only made her look like a bigger badass.

"Uh, yeah." Krys was reminded that she was there to get something taken care of when a kitten bit her thumb. "I called earlier about the kittens? They ain't got no owner, and I'm worried they might have some smoke damage in their lungs. Just little guys, you know?" Their lungs were probably the size of Krys's fingertip. Granted, she had pretty big fingers, but that meant nothing when it came to filtering air!

Siobhan craned her head up and peered into the box. "How many?"

"Four. Keep counting them to make sure they're all there."

Finally, Siobhan kicked herself out of the doorway and motioned for Krys to come in with the kittens. "Bring them on in and we'll have a look at 'em. Tell me what you can."

Krys spilled everything she knew, which wasn't much. By the time she placed the box on an exam table in a tiny room with only one window, she had said everything there was to say. While Siobhan sprayed something on a bath towel and draped it across the table, Krys said, "Thanks so much for doing this. I didn't wanna take them to Dr. Global because..."

"It's all right. I don't have any other critters here right now, let alone something that might like a tasty kitten for a snack." Siobhan placed a stethoscope around her neck, washed her hands, and pulled gloves up to her wrists. Between those and the wire-rim glasses now gracing her face, she looked like any other doctor from the area. *She ain't no Brandelyn Meyer, though.* All right, so they were both intimidating as hell to be around, but Krys always got through her appointments with Dr. Meyer by reminding herself that she was a damn firefighter. If she could stand in the face of flickering flames, she could handle a pretty lady sticking her hand up her shirt – to listen to her heartbeat, of course.

"Do me a favor and put these on." Siobhan tossed Krys another pair of gloves. "With four of the buggers, I might need a little help."

Krys slipped the gloves over her hands, one eye always on the box of fun currently scooting along the exam table. Two of the kittens had taken to throwing themselves against one side of the box, as if they *knew* their mother awaited them over the far edge of the table. *Don't think you're gonna find much down there but a big bump on the head.* At least they were in the right place for it. "I don't have any training beyond some EMT stuff. I can put an oxygen mask on a dog, but that's about it."

Siobhan snapped a surgeon's mask against her face. Was she expecting these cats to carry the next plague? Should Krys be wearing a mask? Or was she already doomed? "You don't need anything a competent layman couldn't accomplish." She lowered her mask far enough to expose her upper lip. "You're a competent layman, right?"

"Prefer laywoman, if it's all the same." Jeez, could she turn up the smarm any more? *This isn't the kind of woman you make "hey! Notice me! As a woman!" jokes around.* Siobhan could perfectly tell that Krys was a woman of a certain persuasion. What did that make Dr. O'Connor? Was she attached? Did she have a husband? A wife? Boyfriend? *Girlfriend?* Krys was usually on top of her gaydar, but that day had already been a wild ride. Between the fire and these kittens, the last thing she expected was discovering a woman like Siobhan living in Paradise Valley. *This might be the first time in several months I've got the hots for someone.* Here she thought she was entering a new phase of her life. One where the hormones finally settled the hell down and she could focus on other things beyond dating, drinking, and fighting fires. *I've already cut back on the drinking.* Since hitting thirty, Krys had discovered she couldn't pound the beers like she used to. She still wasn't sure how she felt about that.

She knew how she felt about this veterinarian, though.

"Hey, did you hear me?"

Krys snapped to attention. A kitten was already halfway into her hand. "No... no, sorry. I'm still a bit weird after the fire earlier. Takes some time to decompress, you know..."

"Less fantasizing, more attention on the cats. We've got four of them to examine, and I'm gonna make sure it's done right."

Krys didn't know what she expected when she brought the kittens here. Dropping them off and leaving? Giving a report? Watching the vet do her work before heading out? Asking what she could do to help them get adopted? It certainly wasn't this. Krys Madison had not woken up that day to meet a pretty veterinarian and cuddle kittens in the clinic with her.

Or maybe she had, and she simply didn't know it yet.

One by one the kittens were weighed, inspected, and checked for fleas and ticks. At the announcement that all four of them were flead the hell up, Krys took a giant step back. Siobhan could only laugh.

"Fleas are everywhere, especially around here. Bet you have some in your house."

"Oh, hell no," Krys said. "My roommate is kinda gross, but not that gross."

"You'll be fine. It's these guys I'm worried about." Siobhan withdrew a cream from one of her drawers. On second inspection, she tossed it back in and grabbed another. "Especially if I'm trying to give them adult formula and not kitten. Their little systems are shocked enough."

Krys knew next to nothing about de-fleaing kittens. She barely knew anything about grown cats. Dogs? Sure. She had a dog with fleas before. Took multiple doses of whatever flea medication was the hot thing ten years ago to get rid of it. *Back when I was a blushing twenty-year-old.* Any fantasies she entertained about owning a dog now were gone with Siobhan's gloves in the trash.

"So, now what?" Krys scratched the back of her head. *Oh, God, I ain't got fleas now, do I?* How quickly could fleas transfer from a kitten to a grown woman? Was what Siobhan said about fleas being everywhere true? What if Krys picked them up in the woods where she found these guys? "I can't really take them home with me. We have a no pet policy at my place."

Siobhan shrugged, as if she hadn't expected Krys to do anything. "I can keep an eye on them for a few days. I've got connections in some shelters around here. Kittens this young are fast adoptions. Granted, they're a little young to be totally weaned and eating solid food, but I don't think I need to bust out the eyedroppers."

Krys paled. "I hadn't thought of that."

"You did the right thing bringing them to a vet. Real shame to hear they don't have their mother anymore, but better for them to come to us early when we can socialize them and get them adopted before they become totally feral. My aunt lives with me. She loves cats. Bet she'll be out here half the night looking after them." Siobhan chuckled. "Probably end up adopting the whole lot of them. Our other cat will *love* that."

Krys couldn't tell if that was sarcasm. "Again, thank you. I looked for a mama cat, but didn't find one. Honestly, I found them in that box there, far away from the barn fire."

Siobhan tapped her finger against her chin. "Suspicious, isn't it? The farmer said they're not his?"

"Said he had never seen them before."

"Still possible they were his barn cats. He just didn't know they were there. That's pretty common. I'm always finding litters of kittens in barns. Go in to check out a horse, come out carrying kittens the farmer doesn't want in his barn."

It's the fact they were in a box that makes it sound suspicious. As if someone knew there would be a fire and made sure nothing was killed. An arsonist with a little conscience? Go figure. *Still something for the fire marshal to figure out.* Krys would be on hand for an interview if necessary, but beyond that, her work was done when the chief pulled them from the scene.

"Tell you what." Siobhan threw out her mask and washed her hands again. Krys lined up behind her to have a turn. "You'll get first dibs to adopt one or all of them if you want. Finders keepers, right?"

"I guess."

"Don't worry about them having owners. Cats get dumped all the time."

She had such a cavalier way of saying that. Was that a byproduct of being a country vet for so long, or was Siobhan sarcastic by nature? It would explain why Krys hadn't ever seen her around town before. *I would remember her, too. A face like that... hair like that... uh, a body like that...* Siobhan was all lean muscle and a few carefully placed curves. Nothing that made her a pin-up model, but she was physical, wasn't she? Country vets were probably like that, always climbing around farms and dealing with big, unruly animals. *I make it sound like she wrestles pigs every day.* Well, maybe she did...

"So..." Krys soaped up her hands while Siobhan dried hers a few feet away. "You've been here a while, huh? I've never seen you around."

What was that look for? Was Siobhan the type to take offence if nobody noticed her? Or was she put out that Krys's nosiness was getting the best of her? "I don't get out much," Siobhan grumbled. Then, "That's not true. I get out a *lot*. Every day, really! I don't go into town much. All of my clients live on farms or up in the hills. Just earlier today I was checking on Rita Mills's cat she found ran over in the road."

Krys searched her memory for that name. *Rita Mills... Rita Mills...* Nope. Didn't ring any bells. Maybe Siobhan was the person most connected to the county's agoraphobic residents. Krys didn't meet people unless they were often in town or constantly calling the fire department.

Or she dated them. Ahem.

"Sorry. Don't know her."

"I know you, though."

Krys patted her hands dry with a paper towel. "Excuse me?"

"Krys Madison. Paradise Valley's only female firefighter. I've had a few friends who dated you."

"Not sure what to say about that." Krys would blush, though. "I've dated a few women over the years, so I couldn't really guess who."

"Yeah." Siobhan turned to the box of kittens. "I know."

How was Krys supposed to take *that?*

"I've got it from here, thanks. Unless there's something else you need?"

Krys was at a loss for words. *Wouldn't mind asking you out.* Yet she was off her game, and she couldn't say why. Lack of practice? Or was there something about Siobhan O'Connor that threw her off, as if Krys had finally met her match in a woman who probably wanted nothing to do with her? *"I've had a few friends who dated you."* Was that said in jest, or anger? Who were these friends Krys had dated? Did things end sourly on one end, and that's what Siobhan had heard over the years? How much was Krys's honor at stake?

"No, it's good." Krys made sure she had everything – minus the kittens, for they were still falling over each other in their box – before heading to the door. "Unless there's anything else you need from me."

Siobhan glanced between Krys and the kittens, a confused smile twitching on her freckled face. *Oh, my God. I'm such a sucker for freckles.* There weren't enough girls with freckles in Paradise Valley. Too many Scandinavians, not enough Irish. "I said I got everything from here. Four kittens, all with fleas but otherwise fine."

"If I hear anything about their owner, I'll let you know."

"You do that."

Krys shut the door behind her and helped herself back out to her car. She lingered by the driver's side door, fumbling with her keys. She was in no hurry to get inside. What if Siobhan suddenly remembered something and needed to talk to Krys a little longer?

Surprise. No such thing happened.

Chapter 4

SIOBHAN

Krys Madison. Go figure.

That was all Siobhan could think about as she and her aunt Gabriella settled the furry children into the comfiest cage in the office. They kittens were *just* small enough that they could realistically climb through the lowest bars and tumble a few yards to the floor. For a grown cat, that was nothing, but for little babies in their tiny, growing bodies, Siobhan was taking no chances. Like she took no chances with a flea bath and the vitamin-enriched food she and Gabriella fed them later that night.

Krys. Freakin'. Madison.

"Aren't they the cutest little floofer-snoofers?" Gabriella was already smitten with every kitten. She went as far as to guess their sexes before her niece had the chance to look. *"Two boys and two girls! Perfect!"* she had exclaimed. She had also become instantly attached to one of the fluffiest kittens, a young female with a white belly and gray coat. Granted, all the kittens were white and gray with similar markings, but this one? The little girl? She was the fluffiest of the whole litter. Big, blue eyes were already the subject of many pictures. "Can we keep them, Chevy? Can we?"

One would never guess that Gabriella was twenty years older than her niece from the way she begged. "I don't know how Clawdette would feel." Their black cat was very much a loner. The whole reason they brought her home from another clinic was because the doctor confessed she had been there for a year, but her anxieties meant she needed a house with no kids or other animals. *Sounds like my place.* Unless these fluffer-nutters came into the main house once they were given a clean bill of health.

"Clawdette is a big girl now," Gabriella said with a sniff. "Come on. These babies need a mama. I can be their mama."

Gabriella's big heart made her a great addition to the softer side of the business. As long as she wasn't around for the harder, sadder parts of the job, she was fine. Yet it also meant moments like these happened. A lot. *If it were up to her, we'd have five dogs, sixteen cats, five birds, and a garage full of gerbils and hamsters.*

"Let's see how it goes with them first, huh?" They were still young enough that anything could happen. Considering the stress they had been through already in their short lives... ugh. Siobhan didn't want to think about it. But if she had to do it, she would. That was part of her job. One of the things she signed up for when she insisted on hundreds of thousands of dollars in debt for vet school.

Gabriella was content to coo over the babies as she fluffed them up a bed made of clean blankets and towels doused in Feel-A-Way. Siobhan knew better, though. Her aunt plotted something in that calculating mind of hers. "So, what did you think of that lady who brought them in? She looked pretty. Uh, single, that is. Pretty single."

Siobhan pretended she hadn't heard anything. A convenient excuse to go check on the drinking water filter arose. It wasn't enough. Once Gabriella latched onto something, she kept at it.

"Did you hear me, Chevy?"

"Yeah. I heard you."

Gabriella wrinkled her nose. "No need to be sound like that. You must know something about her that I don't, though."

"Who? Madison?" Siobhan snorted. "I know you don't know much about it, but she's one of the biggest playgirls in town. Has a different girlfriend every month, if you can believe it." *In a town that small, anyway. Who knew there were enough women to date?* "She pounces on newbies as soon as they roll into town."

"Sounds like you've already dated her!"

"No, but I know somebody who has."

"Who?"

Siobhan looked up and met her aunt's eyes. Gabriella tilted her head until it finally sank in. "No," she said with an exasperated gasp. "You've gotta be kidding. Not..."

"Yup." Siobhan picked up the last of the kittens and placed it with the brothers and sisters looking up at them with big, baby eyes. The cage soon shut in their faces. Gabriella stuck a finger through the bars for one of the kittens to sniff and lick.

"This Madison lady wasn't the one who..."

"I don't think so." Siobhan snapped her work bag closed. "Does it matter, though? It's for the best that I don't have anything to do with her."

"So you admit she's cute?"

"Says the woman who doesn't appreciate women like that."

"I don't have to be gay to know when one of the butchest women to roll up to our house is *good looking.*" Gabriella withdrew her hand from the cage. "She's basically your type, isn't she?"

Siobhan shut off the lights – except for the one by the kittens – and led her aunt out of the office. "I don't have a type," she insisted. "Unless you count someone with integrity."

Gabriella looked after her with *that* look. The same one she always had when they faced Siobhan's past. "You can't stay hung up on that forever, hon. At some point, you're gonna have to move on. It's been three years."

"Not long enough, if you ask me."

That was Gabriella's cue to drop it. By the time they reached the house, stomachs growling and heads full of fatigue, Gabriella went off to heat up some instant dinner and Siobhan collapsed on the couch in front of the TV.

Don't bring her up. Yet did her aunt spare a moment to think about what she should or shouldn't say in front of Siobhan? Some thoughts should be kept to one's self. Like thoughts about a certain someone who moved here to Paradise Valley with Siobhan.

Emily. Go on. Say her name. Emily House. The love of Siobhan's life.

The breaker of hearts, in the worst ways.

How long had it taken for Emily to cheat on her once they were in "paradise?" Four months?

Six months? *Only if I'm being generous.* From the moment they strolled into town four years ago, Siobhan knew it had been a mistake. Apparently, the only thing keeping Emily from cheating on her for the three years they had been together was a lack of opportunity. When nobody else queer enough to sleep with was around, Emily was great! Romantic, attentive, and willing to plan a future with her doting partner. *She got me through school. She got me through some of the worst parts of my life.* Like her father dying, and her grandmother suffering that terrible stroke that left her living in a home.

Then they moved to Paradise Valley. It was supposed to be their forever home, the place that shaped their future marriage and the kids they were gonna have together. *You know, as soon as we settled into our careers. Because that totally happens when you're a vet.* Emily had been quick to agree to buying this house and garage in the countryside for Siobhan to convert into her business. Only a few months later did Siobhan realize their isolation from civilization made for the perfect cover – one in which Emily ran off with half the women around town, sometimes simply drinking up a storm or gambling a little too much money at poker...

And, other times, sleeping with them.

With Siobhan staying out of the town's eyes, most of the women Emily fooled around with probably hadn't known she was taken. That's what cheaters did, after all. They lied about the missus at home. They came up with excuses. *"Oh, well, we're separated. We have an open relationship. She's asexual and allows me to sleep around. Isn't that nice of her?"* None of those things were true. Not even the *nice* part, because as soon as Siobhan found out about Emily's cheating ways, someone's bags were packed and tossed into the county road.

I had never been so humiliated in my life. Siobhan definitely didn't show her face around town now. Why the hell would she, when she might bump into one of Emily's conquests?

That's why she didn't want Krys hanging around any longer than she had to earlier. Not only did some of her mannerisms and personality remind Siobhan of Emily, but she was about 99% certain that Emily had cheated on Siobhan with Krys.

Why wouldn't she? Everyone – and if Siobhan knew, that meant everyone knew – could attest that Krys was a playgirl. Of the monogamous kind, but that was hardly better than someone who played the field. She was one of the first people Siobhan heard about when she moved to there and attended a new people meet and greet at city hall. "*Ooh, watch out for Krys there. From the fire department, you know? Everything they say about them is absolutely true. Lots of muscles, lots of sass, and lots of fun in the sack!*"

That warning was intended to keep Krys from flirting with them. Well, she apparently flirted with someone. It simply wasn't Siobhan.

Did Krys know? Did she have any idea? Was that why she kept acting like an awkward turtle around Siobhan? *She must have known who I am. Acting like she's never seen me before. She had to know.*

Yet what if she didn't?

What if Siobhan had to admit she was into the woman who came rolling up to her door with a box full of kittens.

Freakin' Gabriella was right when she said Krys was totally Siobhan's type. She had the self-assuredness and candor that Emily used to have. Was waaaay more masculine-of-center than Emily, but the ex wasn't exactly femme, either. *I don't know what she was. All I knew was that I loved her.* Seeing Krys reminded Siobhan of something she hadn't thought about in a long while.

How much I wish I had someone.

It was pointless, though. Siobhan was too busy and too isolated from town to have a proper dating life. She barely got cell phone reception out here, let alone decent internet that didn't come from an expensive satellite. Online dating was out of the question. So was popping into the gay bar on weekends. That's what Emily was apparently doing for half the time she and Siobhan were still together in Paradise Valley. *That's probably where she met*

Krys. Everyone (that same everyone from before) knew she hung out there with her best friends. Everyone also knew that she used to date one of those friends.

Player. That's all Krys was. When a woman was a damned firefighter who also looked the part, it only served that she be a big ol' player, too. She could get almost any woman she wanted. Didn't matter if that woman was single or taken, apparently.

Of course she can. When you look like that... God, did anyone else in Paradise Valley have muscles like those? Krys wasn't *ripped,* but she worked out. A lot. She had abs to eat off and biceps to hang from. If she didn't insist on wearing such tight T-shirts with a sturdy sports bra beneath – yes, Siobhan had noticed – then Krys may have gotten out of there unscathed. Instead, she was followed by lustful eyes. The only reason Siobhan didn't completely turn into a puddle of mush was because she was damn good at turning on the stern doctor who treated abused pet animals without letting her feelings get in the way.

Otherwise, she might have giggled like a girl. A girl desperate enough to flirt with the town floozy.

Kittens. It had to be kittens.

"Chevy!" Gabriella stood above the couch, a TV dinner in hand. "Are we gonna eat dinner or not? I've got yours in the microwave right now. Go grab some baby carrots from the bag so we can eat. I wanna watch TV Land. You *know* I love TV Land."

"Yeah." Siobhan shoved herself up. The scent of instant lasagna almost made her gag. "I'll go get something to eat." Only then did she realize she was about to put her hand in Clawdette's face. The big cat always knew how to be in the most inconvenient spot.

"You all right, Chev?"

"I'm fine."

She wasn't fine. When she wasn't fighting images of Emily in the arms of someone like Krys Madison, she was imaging someone else in that same position.

Someone who looked an awful lot like her, red hair, freckles, and all.

Chapter 5

KRYS

The bar wasn't the rowdiest place on Wednesday nights, but the owner of Paradise Lost always did her best to bring in the bodies. That night's treat was a billiard's tournament that had already begun by the time Krys and her friends showed up for their drinks.

While it wasn't unusual to come on hump day, it wasn't the most common occurrence. Yet Krys's friend Lorri said she had a big announcement to make. *Makes me inclined to show up, I guess.*

"Anyone here wanna shoot some pool?" Krys came up behind her friends and offered a hand to their shoulders. Jalen jumped halfway out of her seat. Lorri merely turned from her beer and rolled her eyes at Krys's grand entrance. "Because I practiced all day at the station and am pretty sure I can whip both of your butts."

"Pass," Lorri said. "You may have been bored, but I was lugging boxes from nine to five. I'm not getting up from this seat until it's time to go home. Or until I have to whizz."

Krys looked to Jalen, whose big puppy eyes were closed as soon as she realized her friend was serious. "Hell, no. I suck at pool. Fact, bet that's what you're countin' on!"

"I ain't gonna stiff you guys of your hard-earned money." Krys shoved herself onto the stool between them and flagged the bartender on duty that night. She ordered the same beer as Lorri, because Lorri had excellent tastes in beer. Unlike Jalen, who always went for the fruitier stuff like she wanted to *mask* the taste of alcohol. "I'm here to drink, and to hear what Lorri wants to so badly tell us."

Come on, the woman was about to burst with her news. Lorri was someone who usually kept her personal life to herself, unless some big money was to be made. Somehow, Krys didn't think that's what was going on. More likely it was something else. Something big involving her domestic partner, Joan.

"Out with it," Krys said, hand wrapping around the beer freshly delivered to her spot.

Lorri waited for the bartender to be out of the way before lowering her face toward her friends. "Joanie's pregnant. For real this time."

Jalen yelped so loudly that they drew attention to themselves. Krys whipped her arm around Jalen's shoulders and slapped a hand over that big mouth. Lorri, however, was nothing but smiles as she soaked in the news that she was finally going to be a mom.

"That's amazing, Lor." Krys released the mumbling mouth in her grasp. Jalen mimicked a giant gasp for air as she sat back up and released a kink from her neck. "For real. It's really happening this time?" Poor Joan had suffered two miscarriages in the past year and a half, but both of those happened in the first trimester. "I had a feeling she was pregnant again. Figured you were waiting to tell us until it was farther along."

"You figured it out?" Jalen laughed. "I had no clue!"

You ain't the most observant lady in town, Jay. "Why else would a woman wear those big frumpy clothes in the middle of a mountain summer? Come on. She was hidin' it."

Lorri was still laughing. "Yeah, we got confirmation we're past the scary part. I mean, anything can happen, but trying a new donor seems to have worked so far. Poor Joanie's still heading toward bed rest, though. Doc doesn't want to take any chances."

Krys slammed one hand on the counter and pulled her friend into a bear hug with the other. "That's amazing. Congrats, you stupid idiot."

Lorri shrugged with an uncharacteristic grin on her face. "Good thing that baby ain't gettin' my genes. Since I'm a stupid idiot, and all."

"Exactly. Joan's got a good head on her shoulders, so maybe there's hope for your new family." Krys matched Lorri's grin. "Can't believe you're having a baby. Things are gonna be different in a few months, huh?" That's what she thought the first time Lorri announced she and Joan were having a baby. The second time, everyone remained hopeful, but didn't allow themselves to get too excited. Now, though... maybe the third time was the charm. Maybe this time next year Lorri would have a baby and these mid-week rendezvouses at the bar would be fewer and farther in between. Assuming Lorri pulled her weight in the parenting. Then again, Joan might not let her! "Between you and Jalen over here flying down to LA to hang out with celebrities, who knows what I'm gonna be doing when you two are so busy."

She hadn't meant to sound down on herself. Krys was fine with being alone. She still preferred having companionship, though. That's why she had a roommate, although she could've had her own smaller place. It was also why she used to date around a lot. *That wasn't about getting married or anything, though.* Krys wasn't opposed to a serious relationship, but the past few years had been more about figuring out who she was and what she wanted to do with her life. Since moving to Paradise Valley from Portland a few years ago, she had determined that small town life was more agreeable to her. Slower pace. Less crime. A sense of community built around the same people one saw every day. *With the exception of pretty vets who never come into town.* Go figure. A woman thought she knew everyone...

"You know we're not moving anywhere, right?" Lorri chuckled. "Hell, if we've got a baby tethering us to the house, that means you guys can come over more often. Bring some casserole and we'll let you clean our abandoned bathroom."

Jalen snorted. "I ain't taking care of your babies, Lor. I don't think Krys is, either."

"Who said anything about taking care of the baby Joan's not gonna let go of, anyway? I said bring casseroles and clean the toilet. Ain't that much better?"

"Oh, yeah," Jalen said. "A real hoot. Think I'll be busy."

Lorri shook her hand, as if to smudge the words coming out of Jalen's mouth. Krys merely drank her beer and tried to imagine a Paradise Valley without either of her best friends to hang out with like they always used to. Before, dealing with Lorri's family-making hadn't been too big of a deal. But that was when Jalen was single, too. *At least I had her to keep business as usual, even if Lorri fell off the face of the earth for a while.* Jalen had to go and get that big celebrity girlfriend, though. Fleur was a nice enough lady – *for a Californian* – but if she and Jalen wanted to hang out, it meant Jay left more often. Krys feared that if things progressed with Fleur, Jalen would move away. She may not have any lingering romantic feelings for the woman she dated a while back, but Jalen was still her best friend.

What if Krys was alone at the end of the year?

Things change so quickly in this town. She wondered if small towns were always like this, or if it had to do with the quickly advancing times. People always had somewhere to go and something to do, even if they lived in a quiet little mountain town. Maybe this time next year Krys would be living in Boise, Idaho with a dog and two kids. *Hell if I know at this point!* People came, and people went. Krys simply hadn't thought it might happen so close to home in the span of a few months.

"Like I said," Lorri continued. "Joanie and I ain't moving anywhere. We've got a mortgage! It's Jalen who can't be bothered to hang around anymore."

"What we need to do is get you a real girlfriend. Like what we have, Krys." Ooh, Jalen was loving this, wasn't she? Got a real kick out of being the one with a steady girlfriend before Krys, who used to always have someone to date before she woke up one day and decided to take a break. Jalen had never been as lucky in love, thanks to her awkward demeanor and, quite frankly, lack of natural charisma. She was the pinnacle of country butch who had done her best at school but decided that the tradeswoman life was for her. *I make it sound like I'm so much better than her. I survived community college, but that's it.* Krys had the upper dating hand, though. She was supposed to, thanks to growing up in the city and enjoying more experience with the ladies. Jalen was practically a virgin by the time she moved to Paradise Valley. Or so Krys would go to her grave believing, regardless of what her friend said.

"Seriously, when was the last time you had a girlfriend?" Lorri asked. "Been a while since I heard you talking about someone, let alone saw you strutting around town with a new girl on your arm."

Krys slowly turned her beer bottle around, tracing the logo with her eyes. That soothing motion almost made her forget what Lorri had said. "Told you I was taking a break from dating."

"Yeah, yeah. Admit you can't get a girl for once in your life," Lorri said.

"I'm telling the truth. I could get a date if I wanted. I just wanted to take a bit of a break."

"Uh huh," both of her friends said at the same time.

"I'm serious," Krys grunted. "You guys suck."

Lorri swerved on her stool, eyes rolling with the force of her turn. "It's *okay* to admit that you're going through a dry spell. Happens to everyone, including those in relationships." She gestured to herself. "Look at Jalen. Couldn't get laid to save her life since she stopped dating you, and now she's got the hottest actress in LA in her bed!"

Jalen was almost all grins before she mulled over the first part of Lorri's statement. Meanwhile, Krys was on the brink of uproarious laughter. "I got laid in between! What are you talking about? Don't go spreadin' rumors about me. There was that girl from Junction City who came here for Pride last year. And that lady when I went back to Newport for Christmas. Hey, I'm doing way better than some people around here. You're making it sound like I was one of Krys's charity cases."

"Charity case?" Krys offered her friend a platonic side-hug. *We made awful girlfriends. Thank God it's not weird around here to be friends with your ex.* "No, if you were a charity case, it would've only happened one time. What I'm doing now is a mere blip in my year. I bet I could go out with anyone I want. You know, if they're available."

"Is there anyone around that applies to these days?" Lorri quipped.

"Well..." Krys had been meaning to bring this up, but hadn't the chance. Not with Lorri's big news and Jalen always reminding people that she had Fleur Rose for a girlfriend. "It really pales in comparison to what you guys were talking about, but there may be someone I've been thinking about lately..."

She let her words hang in the air. If there was one thing she had learned about her friends, it was that they needed a hook to get into conversations. No wonder one of them dated a dramatic actress and the other saw drinking her beer as the highlight of her day.

"You gonna tell us or not?" Lorri picked her phone out of her pocket, but it wasn't to make a call or get lost in Facebook. She was the fidgety type that needed something to turn over in her hands or smooth with the pad of her thumb, especially when she was excited. *Daft dunderhead doesn't know she's doing it.* Jalen was two seconds away from ordering peanuts, not that she'd want to eat them. (Most of them she'd foist upon her friends!) She only wanted to crack shells while she laughed and giggled. It was especially bad when they came to watch a game or show on TV. So much wasted money!

Both Lorri and Jalen were giving Krys a look that said she better start spilling before they changed the subject. Right. Now or never.

"Do you either of you know that veterinarian?"

Lorri sat back. "You mean Dr. Global at the animal clinic?" Her wrinkled nose almost made Krys laugh. "That old geezer? That's who you're crushing on?"

"No, no," Jalen interrupted before Krys had the chance to explain. "She probably means that new secretary he has. Had to go in there myself the other day and saw a young lady I'd never seen before. *Really* pretty. But she did have a ring on her hand." Jalen lightly socked Krys in the shoulder. "You chasing married women?"

"Oh, my God, you guys." Krys pinched the bridge of her nose. "Let me finish."

They mimicked zipping their mouths closed.

"Not Dr. Global or anything to do with his clinic. The *other* vet around town. The big animal doc who does farm stuff." Dare Krys drop a name? Act like she personally knew Siobhan as well as it would sound like? "Dr. O'Connor. The lady with red hair."

The lady with red hair. Had a ring to it, huh?

Jalen shrugged. It took Lorri a few more seconds to contemplate Krys's description and figure out who she meant. "Oooh. I think I know her. Comes into the hardware store sometimes. She got the freckles?"

"Oh, yeah. She got the freckles."

Lorri let out a low whistle. "I knew she was a doctor, 'cause it's on her card, but I thought she was some special people doctor. Not animals."

"Yeah, she's got like this barn clinic off the county road. Way outta the way. Had to go up there the other day when I found those kittens in the field."

"You said you took them to the vet..." Finally, Jalen got it. "Oh, you didn't mean Dr. Global."

Lorri was nothing but tittering joviality. "That woman's real mysterious. Barely ever think about her, other than wondering who she might be. She comes into the store about once a month to buy household stuff. Ain't much of a talker. Few times I've tried to figure out where she lives around here, she blew me off and said *out of town.* Real helpful. So, anyway..." She turned to Krys again. "You took her some pussy, and the rest is history?"

"Har, har." That would be the only P-word joke Krys would entertain from these knuckleheads tonight. *Seems so wrong to think that way about her.* They were never above raunchy jokes, especially in the gay bar of all places, but good Lord... that sounded like something that would get Krys's ass kicked if she said it in front of Siobhan. *I'm inclined to stay in her good graces.* She barely knew her, but Krys knew that much. "That was my first time meeting her. Think I spoke to someone else on the phone." Who? Didn't matter.

Someone with a deeper voice. Possibly Siobhan's... partner. Lord, wouldn't that be a hoot? "She's stunning, though. Never seen someone like her around town before. Know anything about her? Like... if she's single?"

Jalen laughed so loudly that she momentarily drowned out the billiard games clacking behind them. "You may be a ladies' woman, Krys, but you're one with morals. Gotta make sure they're single before you put the moves on them."

"Well, yeah. You know I'm not into cheaters. What's the fun in that?" Krys unfortunately knew of women who got off on the forbidden aspect more than they got off on being with another person. Didn't make much sense to her. The whole point of flirting, dating, and getting into bed was the unknown. Would it be great or mediocre? Would you go your separate ways, or would you get married? Which one of you made the better pancakes in the morning? Krys may not have the best track record with long-term dating, but that didn't mean she *hated* the thought. But she definitely wanted a free and open relationship that was out to the world from the moment it happened. Kinda hard to do that if some asshole was cheating. "I figure I've got one more excuse to go see her about these kittens. So, if I'm gonna ask her out, I need to make sure I've got my ducks in a row. Make sure she's not married. Ahem."

"You're not gonna ask if she's gay?" Lorri said.

"First of all, this is Paradise Valley. My odds are pretty good that if my gaydar is going off, she's into women. Second..." Krys puffed herself up, as if she were boasting about her award-winning personality, "I can handle getting shut down because she ain't playing for the home team. It's way more embarrassing for her to tell you she's already got someone, and you probably should have figured that out by now."

Lorri shrugged. "I see her sometimes, but don't know anything about that."

"I've never heard of this lady," Jalen said, "but good luck. Sounds like you might need it for once."

"What's that supposed to mean?"

Jalen and Lorri exchanged a look above Krys's head. "You've been out of the game for a while, right?" Jalen prompted.

"Might be a bit rusty since you last laid it on a woman."

The corners of Krys's mouth twitched. "*Laid it on a woman? You talking about my charms, or my body?*"

"Either's correct, now ain't it?"

Oh, they were really enjoying this. To the point Krys regretted bringing it up. "You guys suck," she said again.

But at least she had alleviated something that had weighed her down since she left Siobhan's property a couple days ago. *She really exists, huh?* Although Krys had searched for Siobhan online, the best she came up with was a website that briefly explained her services. No bells. No frills. Definitely no whistles begging the local farmers and ranchers to call her. She probably worked word-of-mouth, and if she were one of the only house-call vets in the area, landowners had no choice, anyway. Siobhan lived off her business cards, not her website. How many farmers in the area had high-speed internet? Most were so technically illiterate that the fireman joked that at least they knew the fire didn't start because of too many people using their computers at once.

Jalen may have been absolutely worthless for information, but Lorri had known something. She recognized the name, if not the *freckles*. Maybe it was a sign. Krys needed to regroup and think about the best way to ask out the pretty vet.

And maybe ask around a little bit more. Surely, there was someone in Paradise Valley who regularly saw Siobhan when she came into town. Surely. *Someone.*

Anyone?

Chapter 6

SIOBHAN

"Don't forget the dishwashing detergent," Gabriella squawked as she followed her niece down the driveway. Keys jangled from Siobhan's hand. The lights on the truck came on as she unlocked the doors with a push of the button. The door, however, was a bit stuck, because of course it was. Heaven forbid Siobhan make a clean getaway on a day she woke up on the wrong side of the bed.

She may be a bit tetchy because she had to put down someone's beloved herding dog earlier that morning. The poor guy was old, frail, and no longer eating. He had herded his last sheep, and although the family knew it, even the hardest of farmers found it difficult to say goodbye to a beloved pet. Siobhan had the emotional distance to rationalize she was doing what was best for the dog, but when kids started crying and dad slammed his baseball cap on the ground... hard day.

"Yes! Detergent!" Siobhan closed the door behind her. "And the whole laundry list to go with the laundry."

"Sundries, hon." Gabriella said. "We call them sundries."

"Yeah, yeah." Before putting her keys in the ignition, Siobhan dug through a stack of CDs in the hopes of finding something decent to listen to on her drive into town. *Kenny Chesney?* That had to be Gabriella's. *Michael Jackson?* Also Gabriella's. Was there anything in this pile that belonged to...

Ah. Yes. Smashing Pumpkins. Excellent.

Siobhan popped open the case. The *Moulin Rouge!* soundtrack disc fell out.

At least that was also Siobhan's. From when she went through that embarrassing phase in her youth. *Nicole Kidman was my personal goals. Too bad I really don't look anything like her.* Red hair only went so far in the similarities department.

"I'll be back in a couple of hours." Siobhan turned the keys. The truck roared to life. Gabriella took a step back, but did not hustle into the house like Siobhan hoped. "Don't wait up for me."

"You make it sound like you're going on a date!" Gabriella called after her as the truck backed up. "I didn't wake up and see snow, so it must not be a cold day in hell!"

"Bye!"

Turned out it wasn't a *Moulin Rouge!* CD after all. That's what it said on the front, but Siobhan didn't realize until halfway down the driveway that it was a generic P!nk CD with *Moulin Rouge!* written on the front. *Aunt Gabriella strikes again.* This wasn't Siobhan's CD at all. The only time she willingly listened to P!nk was on the *Moulin Rouge!* soundtrack.

To the sounds of "Get the Party Started," Siobhan lowered her sunglasses and bumped over the gravel road leading to the county asphalt. She rolled down her window and hung her elbow out like there was no danger involved. *Like I live life on the edge or something.* Siobhan's idea of a thrill was flying over speed bumps. There was one on the backroad into town, but during that time of year, kids were likely to play in the road. *Never mind.* She had already made one kid cry that day. Like hell she was sending any to the hospital.

There were a myriad of things Siobhan could have done that day. She could have followed up on a few appointments. Done some paperwork. Hell, there was yardwork that needed to be done. Except when she stepped into the shed that day and realized they were out of some gardening materials, Gabriella started a list of everything else they needed from town. Normally, she was the one who ran the errands, but a migraine had knocked her on her ass until the exact moment Siobhan was ready to leave. *That's how it works around here.* Siobhan stopped questioning it when she realized that *avoiding people* was a family trait.

Out on a date... hmph. Yeah, right.

The first stop on Siobhan's tour of Paradise Valley was the biggest hardware store on Main Street. Real Value liked to think it was all that and a bag of nails, but Siobhan often balked at the prices. If gas also weren't so high, she'd save money by driving to the nearest Wal-Mart and taking advantage of their prices. But Real Value was what she got in Paradise Valley, so that's where she went.

"U + Ur Hand" faded into oblivion when Siobhan shut off the engine. *I'll be in and out in ten minutes.* Assuming she found what she needed within ten minutes. Sometimes, the staff at Real Value didn't do their best to stay on top of inventory. How many times had Siobhan suffered through the nuts and bolts, agonizing over sizes and materials? *Only to have the woman who works there tell me she stopped carrying what I needed long ago.*

Great. Siobhan was already worked up before she walked through the door.

Social murmurs greeted her as the bell jingled and the door clasped shut behind her.

The familiar smell of paint, wood chips, and fertilizer greeted her. The concrete floor was shiny enough to reflect her face back up at her, but Siobhan didn't make a point of looking at her feet when around other people. No, her anti-social maneuver was to keep her sunglasses on her head and pretend she didn't notice anyone else.

The saleswoman was "busy" behind the register, yakking away with a customer who didn't look to be buying anything. Just another price one paid when they moved to a small town in the middle of nowhere. Everyone knew everyone, and it wasn't unusual for people to converge in a shop for a long chat that held up lines. Siobhan could only imagine what the line at the post office would be like when she eventually made her way there.

"...Then the guy gets up, shakes us off him, and asks what the hell happened to his car." That's what Siobhan heard as she stopped to check out the fertilizer on sale up front. "You know, the car a few yards away, on fire? The guy was all wet from the spray coming down on us. We had Jaws of Life'd him out only five minutes ago, and all he cared about was the damn car! It wasn't new, man! That thing was junkier than that car in your neighbor's yard."

"You mean the one literally covered in rust and becoming one with the earth beneath it?"

"The very same. It's a miracle that thing didn't spontaneously catch fire sooner than yesterday. We told the guy we were taking him to the county hospital, and he looked at us like we had told him we needed him to come down to the station to sign some forms. Just totally ruined the vibe of his day, you know?"

Small towns. Siobhan shook her head, too distracted to read the weights and ingredients of the bags. *I can't remember what Aunt Gabriella wanted. And she'll lose it if I bring back the wrong fertilizer for her damn flowers.* The vegetable garden, which Siobhan benefitted greatly from, but she wouldn't go that far.

"You sure I don't know this guy?"

"He's not from around here. Think he's from Seaside. Was heading back that way from Portland, anyway."

"It was the Portland that did it to him. Every time I gotta drive Joanie there, I lose another year off my life. It's a damn miracle *our* car hasn't blown up yet!"

"Hey, that's my hometown you're talking about."

"I thought *this* was your hometown now?"

"Don't get snooty with me. You know what I meant."

Were these two friends, or frenemies?

The one taking up the cashier's time stepped back. Finally, the woman who worked there rounded the corner of the counter and approached Siobhan. "Can I help you find anything? All of our fertilizers are on sale this..."

Siobhan barely registered the tall woman in green and black flannel. She was too busy lowering her sunglasses down her nose and seeing the fine person still standing at the counter.

Damn. Those are some serious abs... The woman wore a black windbreaker, but she stood at an angle that showed off the crop top beneath it. *A crop top. In Paradise Valley. Go figure.* No, no... that was a sports bra, huh? A big, bulking sports bra that held down the girls while not leaving much to the imagination. The windbreaker was merely a way to keep prying eyes like Siobhan's away. Not that it was doing much good now.

Only two seconds later did she realize that her knight in gleaming, sweaty armor was Krys Madison. That realization didn't settle in until Siobhan lifted her eyes and caught Krys's in the ultraviolet lights.

Was the acknowledgment instantaneous? Or did Krys give that look to every woman who crossed her path?

"Sorry." Siobhan said to the cashier, before turning back to the fertilizer bags. "Thought I saw someone I know."

She was met with an incredulous look. "Who, Krys over there? You probably do know her. Everybody does."

Krys raised her hand before slapping it back against her hip. "That's right. Everybody knows me. If you've ever been on fire, we've met."

"That's why she walks around town half naked, right?"

"I ain't half-naked, Lor. I'm in a sports bra and sweatpants. I got a jacket on!"

Yes, I can see that. Siobhan's throat was dry. Her *mouth* was dry. If she licked her lips right now, would it look weird? Too desperate? She couldn't claim any attraction to the woman standing a few feet away. For one thing, Siobhan was *not* attracted to Krys. Not like that. She could mentally acknowledge a good-looking woman who checked all the "right" boxes, but it wasn't like she wanted to drool over Krys. *Not when I can think of a few other people who have already.* Even if Emily hadn't gone out with Krys back in those hellish days, it was enough to know that half the town had.

Wait... did Krys not recognize Siobhan? Oh, that was low.

"Hey," Siobhan said. Her pride may be on the line. Yes, even she could be vain enough to get this woman's attention. "Nice sports bra."

"Oh, you like it?" Krys popped open her jacket. Lovely. She had an even tan that suggested she spent a lot of time out in the sun. A people doctor like Brandelyn Meyer would chide Krys for exposing her tender skin to the sun like that, but a vet didn't care as much. *This* vet in particular was too busy averting her eyes so she wasn't caught staring at pectorals. "Had to buy it online. They don't make many good sports bras in my size. Definitely not anywhere around here."

Lorri the cashier threw her hands up toward the ceiling and returned to her station. What did that mean? She didn't think she was gonna help Siobhan now that Krys had her attention? *It's not like I'm running out of here with her!* Although she wished Krys would put a real shirt on. Like the tight T-shirt she wore the other day, when those big, strong muscles brought in a box of mewling kittens.

Oh, God. Someone needed a date.

"A good bra can be hard to find," Siobhan agreed. She may not have been super well-endowed, but she was picky about underwires and frilly lace on her underwear. "Luckily, you seem to have that mystery sorted."

Krys's smile lit up the whole room. Did she know she had mega-watt teeth? Or did she ooze flirtations as easily as she breathed? *Does she know what power she has over women?* Power over women. Yeah. That was it. Totally not sexist or toxic at all. "Dr. O'Connor, right? Sorry, I didn't really recognize you at first with the glare coming through the window."

Someone rolled her eyes with an exasperated sigh. It was neither Krys nor Siobhan.

"Yes, that's me."

Krys stepped away from the counter, "How are those kittens doing? Been thinking about them ever since I dropped them off at your place."

"Hey," Lorri interrupted, with a rap of her knuckles against the counter. "I gotta go bring some stuff out from the back. Let me know if you need anything, though." That was said to Siobhan, who was still technically a customer, even if she played a game of Small Town Small Talk in the hardware store.

"The kittens are fine." *Really, you're asking me about kittens?* She supposed that was the safest conversation starter. "Playing a bunch, eating their food, and growing like they should. They'll be ready for adoption as soon as I confirm they no longer have worms."

Krys wrinkled her nose. "Worms, huh? First it's the fleas..."

"Don't worry. I hardly doubt you caught anything from them. You would've, ah... known by now."

"I'll keep that in mind."

The awkward silence finally came. Siobhan didn't know if she should turn back to the fertilizer and pretend she didn't see Krys, or wait for Krys to say farewell and head out the door.

Krys wasn't moving.

Well, she was *moving,* but she was coming closer to Siobhan instead of the door.

Great! Exactly what I want on my first foray into town all month! Siobhan had an excellent poker face, but that was the only thing she had going for her. Krys might not know that Siobhan's heart was thumping like crazy inside of her chest, but damnit, *Siobhan* knew. She continued to rationalize that physical attraction was perfectly acceptable. She couldn't help whom she was attracted to, like she couldn't help the crack in her voice when she attempted to speak. That didn't mean she followed through on attraction, though. That was the difference between her and Emily. *Is it natural to be attracted to people? Duh. Does that mean you go around sleeping with people? Kick your ass if you're my girlfriend...*

Krys was one of those people who knew she didn't have to settle, huh? She could date around all she wanted because she had a body like that and knew how to use it to her advantage. She lived in a haven for lesbian dating and didn't worry about who to make her next girlfriend. There was nothing special about Siobhan, beyond the novelty of her identity. Krys flirted with everyone. Even her friends.

Thinking that made it easier to stand so close to her. With her abs hanging out. Yup.

"You know, that wasn't the only person I was thinking about..." Krys said. "Been thinking about you too, Dr. O'Connor."

Although Siobhan expected it, she couldn't hold back the rolling of her lips as she attempted to quash a smile of girlish excitement. *Come on! Who doesn't want to be flirted with like this?* All Siobhan had done was go into town to run some errands. Next thing she knew, the hottest woman she had ever seen in Paradise Valley was walking around with her muscles hanging out and a smirk on her face. Was it really reserved for Siobhan? Or would Krys have hurled it at whoever came her way next?

"Is there a Mrs. O'Connor?" Only Krys could ask that and not sound too cheesy to bear. "Or a Mister, for that matter? I gotta get my story straight before I try asking you out."

Siobhan placed both hands on her hips, her handbag sliding off her shoulder and looping around her elbow. Sure, she would have *loved* to put that bag down and not look so ridiculous, but she refused to lose balance in front of Krys Madison. Especially when Ms. Madison was coming onto her stronger than a cup of black coffee.

"I'm not married," Siobhan said. "Nor am I looking for anybody to date." That was the most diplomatic thing she could say. Siobhan was also careful to avoid pronouns, if only to drive Krys a little crazier.

"All right." Krys held up her hands. "No worries. I can take a hint."

"What hint?"

"Uh, the hint that you don't wanna grab a coffee with me sometime?"

"You greatly overestimate my desire to socialize with people."

"Hey, I get it. That's a long drive into town from where you live. I wouldn't be in a hurry to head here for little ol' me, either." Krys shrugged, one sleeve of her windbreaker sliding off her shoulder. *That's not fair.* She might as well walk around in a crop top, after all. "But I thought I'd at least ask about the kittens."

"Your convenient segue into asking me out?"

"I care about those worm-infested fleabags. Think I would've brought them in if I didn't?"

Who's paying for their care, anyway? Oh, right. Me. Sometimes, Siobhan was a charity.

When she could afford it, anyway. "Your heart is truly big. I can see that." She didn't keep her eyes off that cleavage peeping at her. Smooshed cleavage, but hey, those were breasts under there. Siobhan knew how to appreciate those, especially when it had been three years since she was last intimately familiar with a pair.

"I'm also told I have a pretty big ego to go along with my hunk of hubris." Krys kept a respectful distance from Siobhan, but she may as well have lunged for a kiss from the force soon felt in that little corner of Real Value Hardware Store. "Some people may not be into that, though. I respect that."

Do you respect other people's partners, too? Every time Siobhan thought about lowering her defenses a tad, she remembered what happened with Emily. The betrayal. The hurt. The loneliness. Maybe Krys was innocent in all aspects. Maybe she was guilty, and knew. Either way, could Siobhan live with herself for *enjoying* Krys's company, let alone wanting to go somewhere with her?

"I'm not really looking for a date right now."

"Who said it had to be a date?"

How smooth. Make it sound like a friendly flirtation and nothing more. "Well," Siobhan began, "unless you have something specific to invite me to, it definitely sounds like a date."

"Hm. Maybe... I simply want to hang out with those cats a little longer."

And I want to come to the firehouse to slide down the pole. Siobhan wondered if she could actually do that. Specifically, the firehouse pole. Not Krys's pole. Nope. Siobhan wasn't about to accidentally say that at all.

"They do need more human socialization," Siobhan said with a little squeak. "My aunt is all over them, but she has more work to do around the place. I mean, it's not impossible for someone to come all the way out there to pet them, feed them, and talk to them. Will make it easier to adopt them out when they're ready."

"Is this before or after you spay and neuter the poor dears?"

Siobhan chuckled. "Hopefully, I won't have to do that. Better for that to be someone else's responsibility."

August Heat

"What if I took up a collection around the firehouse? To pay for their fixing?"

Although Siobhan still laughed, she didn't know why. Was what Krys said really ridiculous? Or was it because Siobhan *knew* it was a ploy to woo her? Krys couldn't be serious about having a "heart" big enough to pay for four kittens to get fixed. Because Siobhan couldn't do it on her own, and her aunt wasn't certified to administer medications, let alone assist in surgery. Siobhan could fix a cat in her sleep, but she rarely did it. Rather, she referred those patients to Dr. Global or someone else with a proper clinic and vet techs to assist them. The only surgeries Siobhan performed on pets were emergencies, and she still preferred to have at least one other doctor there with her. Hell, she'd take Dr. Meyer over her own aunt!

"If you manage that, I'm sure Dr. Global would help. I could take them over myself."

Krys tilted her head. "Hey, if you don't want me around, say so."

Yes, please stay away, troublemaker. Let me stew in my loneliness. "It's easier for me to do it. I know the other vets around here pretty well. We do talk, you know." Not super willingly. When Siobhan wasn't holing herself away from the world, she was avoiding the town vet at the post office. Dr. Global *loved* to say hello and "shoot the farm animal breeze" with her. Siobhan had a hunch that he had aspired for a career more like hers instead of a private practice that took care of the Fluffies and Rovers of a small town. There was arguably more money in it, though. Siobhan lucked out that big animal doctoring often meant living in cheaper places.

"Like I said," Krys continued with a lackadaisical smile, "if you don't want me around, just say so."

Siobhan narrowed her eyes. *What game is she trying to play with me?* Everything depended on whether Krys knew about Emily. If she did, then this was a sick joke. If she didn't, then Siobhan had more than egg on her face – she had a whole damn omelet.

"How about I come by tomorrow? Or the day after tomorrow?" Krys winked before turning around. "Like you said, the little furballs need some socializing before they turn feral."

"Not quite how I put it." The kittens weren't in real danger of "turning feral" now, but the extra human socializing would make them better for adoption. Dare Siobhan admit that, though? "If you insist, may I request you wait until the late afternoon? I'm usually away during the mornings, and God only knows what calls I might get through the day. Besides, my aunt might not know who the hell you are and let you in to see the babies."

"Who's your aunt? I know almost everyone around here."

Siobhan was about to ignore that question, but realized that there was no use hiding it now. Gabriella O'Connor. You might have seen her around town. She's usually the one running the errands." *And trying to have a social life.* Short of joining the Stephen King book club or one of the quilting circles, though. Aunt Gabriella was looking at a long life of nothing.

"Right. Tomorrow. Or day after tomorrow. Afternoon." Krys backed toward the door. She didn't dare turn around, huh? Because then Siobhan would miss out on more of those abs, and Krys couldn't have that. She was on a mission to show the whole world how trim and athletic she was. So everyone could rest assured that she'd bail them out of their next fire. "See you there." That was *supposed* to be a devilish wink, but Krys backed her ass up against the push bar of the door. Siobhan tried not to laugh as Krys stumbled out the door and acted like she had meant to do that. Her friend Lorri, however, openly guffawed behind the register.

"Hope she didn't bother you, ma'am!" Lorri called. "Though if you say the word, I'll make sure she gets a good talkin' to."

Siobhan was good at acting like she hadn't noticed anything about Krys's heavy-handed flirtations. *Heavy-handed... would most people think that?* Or did Siobhan see the worst in everyone's intentions?

"No worries. My only real care is about fertilizer, if you don't mind."

Lorri hurried out from behind the register. She may have enabled her friend, but at least she was good at pointing out the best fertilizer for Gabriella's vegetable garden. Wasn't that the only thing Siobhan cared about?

...Supposedly?

Chapter 7

KRYS

You've got this. Why the hell are you so nervous about playing with some kittens?

Krys took five minutes to transition from her car to the O'Connors' driveway. Both Siobhan's truck and the family car were parked by the garage. A colorful flag waved from the porch of the main house. Plastic windmills twirled in the small beds of flowers. Windchimes shuddered in the breeze and trees rustled overhead. It looked like a cozy piece of country living, but Krys's anxiety grew as she approached the giant white shed by the vehicles.

She knew when she liked a woman, and she *liked* Siobhan. Those red curls were barely tamable by the ponytails Siobhan put them in, but those freckles didn't stand a chance once the sun was free from the clouds. Whether she wore baggy clothes or something more tasteful, Siobhan was a confident sight to behold. Krys was always a sucker for confident, feminine women who didn't care if they got their hands dirty. While Krys would never say she preferred butch over femme when it came to dating and lovemaking, she definitely needed a partner who embraced the "tomboy" level at some point in her life. Whether that meant climbing trees at seven, playing softball in high school, or riding a Harley as an adult... it was the attitude that mattered most. Krys's most memorable girlfriends were those who didn't mind some mud on their boots. Hair length and choice of skirt or cargo shorts didn't make any difference.

She shoves her arms up barnyard animals' asses, so... Krys assumed Siobhan washed up.

That's not why she was so nervous, though.

I don't think she likes me very much.

Krys didn't see that as a challenge. If anything, it hurt her to know that someone she barely knew didn't think too highly of her. Had Krys done something? She had come on too strong. That was the problem. Lorri and the others were always telling Krys that she couldn't run up to every pretty lady and ask them out like it was another day ending in Y. *Maybe I'm off my game. It's been how long since I asked someone out?* Krys approached the office door and knocked. *I'm not as suave as I used to be. This is it. This is what it's like to become a dating has-been.*

The door opened. Siobhan blocked the entryway, her hair pulled back into a loose ponytail that continued to take up more space than her shoulders. Or the big lab coat that draped over her tank top and khaki capris.

"So..." Siobhan's eyes darted up and down the length of Krys's body. She wasn't so much checking Krys out as she was... what? Sizing her up? Making assumptions based on how well Krys took care of her body? "You came. To play with my kittens."

"I'm assuming that was actually okay. You didn't say I couldn't, so I..."

Siobhan stepped away. "They're in here. Just woke up from their naps so they should be nice and energetic for you, Ms. Firefighter."

"What are you trying to say?" Krys chuckled as she shut the door behind her. An air conditioner worked in tandem with a standing fan to keep air moving through the small kennels in the back. The kittens were still the only animals in there, which meant Siobhan had released them to run around the enclosed space. Toys littered the floor. Fuzzy strings hung from the exam table. A blanket was piled in the corner, long since abandoned now that four baby animals tussled and mewled. No wonder. The food dish was empty. Somebody had lots of energy.

"Knock yourself out," Siobhan said. "I've got some paperwork from an appointment to fill out in the other room. Let me know if there are any issues."

Krys already had one wiggly kitten in her hands. "You're not gonna help me *socialize* them?" Huh. That was a terrible pickup line. She should try again. "I mean, I would think the more people that do it at once might be..."

"Overstimulation," Siobhan said. "Bombarding someone with too much talking and touching can cause overstimulation, and then you lose all progress."

She said it so quickly that Krys wondered if they were still talking about cats. "Cool. I'll hang out for a while. By the way..." She caught Siobhan before she went into the other room. "I talked to my chief down at the firehouse. He said it's cool if I collect some money to cover the costs for these little guys. You may not believe it, but firefighters are the biggest softies of any emergency response bunch." That wasn't something Krys had ever thought about until now. *It's kinda true, though.* People assumed firefighters got into it because they loved the thrill, the adventure, the *cool* factor of jumping into fires and barely making it out alive. Okay, so maybe that was a part of it. In Krys's case, she had thought about becoming an EMT and putting her empathetic nature to work, but more than one person suggested she had the body and stamina for firefighting. *Here I am, rescuing kittens from the smoldering rubble.* Krys looked down at the squirming furball in her grasp. The kitten was desperate to pounce on his brother, the kitten currently rubbing up against Krys's leg.

"Big softies, huh?" Siobhan asked with crossed arms. "Stop talking about how nice you are and prove it." She closed the door, although a glance through the tiny window assured Krys that Dr. O'Connor was at her desk in the other room.

Krys sat in one of the chairs on the side of the small room and cuddled two of the kittens. They bit her fingers before gingerly licking them. They faked her out by pretending to want belly scritches, only to nip her a moment later. They climbed her shoulders like she was Mt. Everest, and one little girl was brave enough to stand on top of her head and take full survey of her domain. Krys hadn't realized they were old enough to accomplish such feats. *How old is a kitten that is ready to be adopted?* When did they need to be fixed? When did they cross the threshold from adorable kittens to hellacious juveniles? *It's been so long since I've had a pet, and most of them were dogs.* Tomboy Krys knew all about playing outside with dogs. Big labs, little terriers... either kind were good for running, jumping, barking, and swimming. Cats, though? They were sweet, but they weren't what she thought of when she imagined a lifelong pet to go on adventures with, whatever they may be.

I wonder what Siobhan's favorite animal is... She seemed like a horse girl. Didn't most horse girls have dreams of becoming veterinarians and that's how it always began? *I wonder if she's gay...*

Krys didn't think she was such hot stuff that she could have any woman she wanted, but it was strange how Siobhan acted around her. She both knew Krys, yes... knew almost nothing about her. They had never had a conversation before that week. Krys barely recognized her from years of living in Paradise Valley. Siobhan was a hermit who only left her isolated property to go to *other* isolated properties. Her clients were animals, not people. She seemed old enough to not only have life experience, but romantic experiences as well. She lived with an aunt, for God's sake. That didn't scream a woman looking for romance, of either the homo or hetero variety.

Why do I care so much?

Because Siobhan was gorgeous? Intriguing? Fascinating? Krys knew she wouldn't start dating again until the right woman crossed her path. Hm, it had happened, huh? All she had to do was pick up some kittens.

After a while, she stopped thinking so much about Siobhan. When alone with four playful kittens, a woman jumped into the exciting world of babysitting.

It only took her fifteen minutes to define the differences between them. This one had white socks. That one had a giant, prominent black M on his forehead. This one was fluffier than the others, and that one had a short, stubby tail. Now, Krys didn't know anything about sexing cats, but she recalled that two were male and two were female. The hairy one was female. After that? She guessed.

"Look at you guys. Where's your mama, huh?" Krys sat cross-legged on the floor, her lap covered in kittens. "Somebody put you out there in that box. You guys are strong, but you didn't get there on your own. You trying to tell me that's what happened?"

She was met with a chorus of happy meows. The hairy little girl attempted to leap off Krys's lap and instead tumbled to the floor. Krys picked her up and gave her a tiny squeeze. Protests prompted her to put the kitten back down.

"People always be dumping their pets like it's nothing. You guys gotta get fixed so it doesn't happen to any descendants of yours. You know how many cats we've got on this planet? You guys are adorable, but we don't need more of you. That's why I've gotta raise some money to get you guys..."

The one with the prominent M chomped on her thumb. Krys yelped in both pain and surprise.

That was the moment she knew. No, not the moment she was bitten like a toy... the moment she looked down in that kitten's eyes, and he guiltily backed away like he knew he almost ruined a good thing.

"Hey, doc." Krys opened the door, careful to keep the kittens from spilling out the crack. "What if I took the kittens home when they're ready to go? I've got plenty of space in my garage for them to run around. Got some friends who'd love to play with them." Her roommate might raise an eyebrow, but...

Siobhan leaned back in her chair, hands behind her head and fingers digging into her curly hair. "Didn't you say your lease doesn't allow pets on the premises?"

"Not like the landlord makes weekly or monthly inspections. Guy doesn't live in the state anymore. I could totally get away with some smuggled kittens until they're adopted."

Why was Siobhan rolling her eyes? "You really like those kittens, huh?"

"Guess you could say I feel some responsibility. I found them, after all."

"They certainly owe their little lives to you." The vet shrugged her way back into a proper seating position. "I need to clear that place out, anyway. I got a call earlier today about a mama raccoon and her babies making a mess out of somebody's house. Usually first thing people do after trapping them is bring them to me, and I cannot have raccoons and cats in the same room. Hell, I don't want raccoons and bears in the same room."

"Raccoons, huh? That sounds pretty badass."

"What does?"

"You saving a mama raccoon and her little babies. You release them back into the wild?"

"Not usually." A little grin tugged at Siobhan's cheeks. She was somehow prettier when smug like that. "I save that for animal control. Or whoever is doing it these days." She glanced down. "Uh, you're letting the beasts loose."

Krys felt the tiny beast stumbling over her foot before she saw it. Mr. Prominent M had broken free of his large cage, and the first thing on his to-do list was to march in Siobhan's direction. Instead of snatching him up and returning him to his prison, Siobhan cocked her head and clicked her tongue. Two seconds later, he was willingly in her hands.

"So, uh… when should I take the little guys?" Krys asked. "I could take them with me tonight. Hey, might be a great way to pick up a date around town. You know how ladies are about fuzzy animals." *Especially if you don't want to go out with me, Siobhan… might as well find someone to go out with around here.*

Siobhan dropped the maternal visage when Krys said that. "They're living creatures, Ms. Madison. They don't exist for scoring dates and hot chicks."

"Uh, I never said…"

The little boy in Siobhan's hands mewled helplessly as she pressed him against her shoulder and carried him back into the exam room. "I know your type."

That was all she said. It was enough to shock Krys where she stood, conveniently pressed in the doorway. Yet she was as helpless as that kitten to stop the little flood of mewling brothers and sisters coming out of the room. After Siobhan put the male kitten in the kennel, she rushed to grab the others and settle them down for another nap as well.

"Excuse me?" Krys said. "Is this what your problem with me has been?"

Siobhan attempted to shut the door in Krys's face. *Oh, no. I don't think so.* A woman did not slap her with such words and get away without explanation. Krys would jam the door back open and get to the bottom of this, and she didn't care if Siobhan gave her a look of absolute death.

Chapter 8

SIOBHAN

What a blowhard. *What an idiot.* Siobhan had half a mind to ram her foot up Krys's smug ass. *She has got to be kidding me. Coming out all this way to lay the flirtations on me, and when I don't respond? She wants to take these poor kittens and use them as girlfriend bait!* If anyone tried to tell Siobhan that men were always worse than women in the slime department, she'd point to this moment and tell them to sod off.

Certainly, there were women who could be worse. Way worse.

"Did I completely miss something?" Krys snapped. Kittens cowered in their kennel.

Siobhan turned off the light above their heads to give them some extra comfort. Krys continued to bring down the energy behind her. "Have I offended you in some way? I barely know you."

You know me much better than you think. Siobhan locked the kennel and slowly turned to Krys, who barricaded the door with her muscular body and tough-girl demeanor. Siobhan didn't know if she was frightened or turned-on. The indistinction did not give her much confidence, but the embittered rage that had been festering for the past few years did.

"Remember someone named Emily House?"

Krys went from offended to confused in less than a second. Siobhan used that opportunity to shove her hands in her coat pockets and stand up to a bully.

"What?"

Unbelievable. Feigning innocence. Should Siobhan be offended by that, or simply roll with it? "Emily House. I believe you used to date her for a hot minute, like you date so many women around here for such a short time."

Slow realization dawned in Krys's big, brown eyes. She lowered her guard – including her body that continued to barricade the door – and shook her head in apparent disbelief. "What are you on about? So I've dated a few gals. You got a moral problem with that? Lady, you're living in the wrong area."

"I don't care that you date women." A fine thing to accuse her of, since Siobhan wasn't much better. *She doesn't realize I'm gay, does she?* Did Siobhan no longer exhibit the right "vibes?" Oh, too bad. She had left her Double Venus necklace and lesbian flag-colored tank top in her closet. "I care that you don't think twice about the women you do date."

"I'm getting the feeling this Emily woman you're talking about was someone off limits."

Shuddering, Siobhan looked the other way. She wasn't about to gaze into Krys's eyes when tensions rose and they hashed out the drama Krys didn't know existed. "Off limits? You could put it that way. She was my partner."

A shred of sympathy appeared on Krys's countenance. *It's too late. The damage is done.*

"I'm sorry," Krys said. "I don't know who that is. The only Emily I know around here is the lady who helps run the supermarket. I also don't make a point of dating unavailable women. Kinda takes the fun out of it when you know they're cheating on someone."

"I'm pretty sure you dated her." Siobhan scoffed. "I mean, she was a huge, homewrecking jerk, but I don't take too kindly to those who helped her achieve those results."

"Like I said..." Krys lowered her mouth, growl rumbling in her throat. More shudders overcame Siobhan's body, but she couldn't say if they were from the dark memories flooding her mind or that low, deep growl rumbling through her ears. "I don't remember no Emily. I definitely don't remember dating someone who already had someone. If I did, then they never told me. Some people are like that, yeah? They keep their real selves hidden away so nobody can ever find them."

Was that a dig at Siobhan? *You asshole.* She attempted to keep her cool, but anger burned her cheeks. "You don't remember her? Well, she probably doesn't remember you, either, but I remember the both of you pretty well. She ruined everything we had, and did it right after we moved here. I don't care if you knew about her or not. The fact is, I don't..."

"Emily House," Krys repeated, her whole body moving out of the way. She stood in the main office, a little too close to the computer and file cabinets for Siobhan's liking. "How long ago was this? Two years? Three years?"

"What does it matter now?"

"I'm trying to remember, okay? I don't want you going around town thinking I slept with your girl if I really didn't. I've got *some* reputation to protect, you know."

What? That you're easy? No, Siobhan would not say that out loud. "Reputation? I don't care about your reputation. I care that you might have slept with my ex. While she was with me."

God, where was this coming from? Siobhan did *not* dump this on people. She didn't dump it on her aunt! Gabriella had spent years trying to get the whole story out of her niece's mouth, but Siobhan had clamped it down before anyone had the chance to reopen her wounds. *Krys Madison is the last person I would talk to about this. Screw her.* Not literally. Figuratively.

Tears appeared. With shame for herself dripping down her cheeks, Siobhan turned away, the back of her hand covering her face.

"Hey…" How dare Krys sound so soothing right now? Didn't she realize what was going on? She was being accused of stealing another woman's partner! Did that not mean anything to her? "I'm sorry that happened to you. That's a shitty thing to do to somebody you supposedly love. I don't play like that, though. I've dated around a lot, yeah, but that doesn't mean I don't got *some* morals. I don't fool around with cheaters. First of all, that's a dick move. Second of all, why would I want to date someone who cheats? They're just gonna cheat on me, too, right? 'Cause that's what cheaters do. I ain't no cheater, and I try to avoid dating them like they've got the plague. They do, right? They've got a plague that wants to take my sanity down with them."

Siobhan barely understood what Krys said. "Even if you didn't know... I don't flirt with players. So I'd appreciate it if you stopped using these kittens as bait to get to either me or some other woman. They're living creatures, thank you very much."

"Hey." That wasn't the tender, reassuring *hey* from earlier. That was a *"excuse you very much"* kind of *hey*. The snap was heard throughout the whole shed, not that there was anything beyond Siobhan to receive the force in her ears. "I ain't using animals to get to *anybody*. You think I don't care about them? You think this has all been an elaborate rouse to flirt with you and get you to go out with me?" She scratched the back of her head. "Maybe a little."

Siobhan's eyes widened. "Excuse me?" She hadn't actually meant it. Not with any real certainty, since she knew she was another potential notch on Krys's bedpost. She didn't care about *her,* Siobhan O'Connor. *I'm a pretty face for her to fool around with until she's bored.* That's how players operated. That's how

Emily had operated, and Siobhan was well-acquainted with what kind of player *she* was.

Krys was halfway out the door by the time she replied. That take-it-or-leave-it attitude both infuriated and impressed Siobhan, who had expected a more lackadaisical response to her accusations. "Sorry if I got the wrong impression of you. Here I was worried about thinking you were gay when you're really not. Instead, turns out you hold some grudge against me for something I didn't do. My reputation precedes me, as usual."

"Are you saying you *actually* intended to ask me out this whole time?"

"I mean, I like animals, okay? It's not like I scrounged around for some kittens to use to get to you, Dr. I-Never-Met-Before-the-Other-Day. Now I'm not sure I want to ask you out. You seem like more trouble than you're worth."

Siobhan gasped. *That's what I've been thinking about you!*

They were at an impasse. Krys remained in the doorway, but she was in no hurry to leave. Siobhan stared at her as if she were an intruder.

Upon her property? Not as much as she was an intruder upon one woman's bruised soul.

"Ah, what the hell!" Krys flung herself against the doorframe, eyes rolling up toward the ceiling as she smacked a hand against the wall. "You wanna go out sometime? Dinner? Movie at the park? I hear they're playing *But I'm a Cheerleader* this weekend. You know you wanna go. With me." She cleared her throat, a flicker of doubt betraying that exuding confidence. "How's that? Is it working?"

Siobhan had such dire whiplash from that spiel that she clutched the back of her office chair. "I... I have never seen that movie. So I don't know if I want to see it or not."

"So... you haven't seen it before..." Krys flicked her fingers down toward the floor. "That means you should go..." They slowly raised again, index fingers pointing while the rest balled into a fist. "With me." Both tips of Krys's index fingers jammed into her chest.

Siobhan could only gape at her.

"That's how it works." Krys sniffed, resuming the stance of a woman who knew how to get a date. "You have not seen an iconic lesbian movie. That means you need to come with me to go see it. What time am I picking you up Saturday night?"

The chair squeaked beneath the pressure of Siobhan's knee. "What time does it start?"

"Eight, I presume."

"That's kinda late..."

"What? You work on Sunday mornings?"

"Sometimes. If I get a call. Farm animals don't wait to get sick or injured, you know."

Krys grinned. "Hey, if you hate the movie, you can leave early."

Siobhan weighed those options while Krys continued to linger in the doorway. The slamming of a door in the distance meant the oncoming nosiness of one Aunt Gabriella. Siobhan had to think fast, Preferably, to rid herself of this nuisance clogging up her office. "I'll drive into town around 7:30. If I think you've picked out a decent spot, I might hang around. For cinematic purposes, of course."

Brows knitted and body backing out of the doorway, Krys said, "Of course. Cinematic purposes." The door was half closed when she poked her nose in again. "Saturday night. Eight. The park in town."

"I'm sure I'll find it." There was only one park in Paradise Valley, and only one lawn big enough to host a "movie in the park" premier. Siobhan would be lucky to find parking, though. She had been there when a T-Ball game happened, and it was *not* good.

She didn't go after Krys when the door shut and a car engine started a minute later. Glares from Krys's car reflected off the office windows. They prevented Siobhan from seeing her aunt open the door, giving her the start of her life.

"Who was that, huh?" Gabriella took another look in Krys's direction. "You know I don't swing that way, but that gal has a *nice* ass."

"I hear that's what happens when you're a firefighter." Siobhan cleared her throat and flicked the hair out of her face. She did *not* need her aunt beholding how flustered some people in that office were. "You get a nice ass."

"Oh? Firefighter, huh?" Gabriella leaned out the door, right foot hovering in the air as she got a good, long look of the old car disappearing down the driveway. "Then again, if that's what the firefighters look like around here, I might have to start dating around. Friend of yours?"

Siobhan finally succumbed to her squeaky office chair. "She's helping with the kittens. She's the one who brought them in."

"And?"

That got Gabriella a harsh look over the shoulder? "And what?"

"Aaaaand?"

"And we might be seeing the movie in the park on Saturday," Siobhan muttered.

Too loud, apparently. That gave Gabriella the ammunition she required to grab Siobhan by the back of the chair and spin her around like it was her birthday. Gloats that it was "about time someone went on a date again" filled the air.

Siobhan felt like she was about to be sick. The spinning chair wasn't the only culprit.

Chapter 9

KRYS

"Hear me out, would you?" Krys placed her elbow on the chief's desk, coffee-stained papers rustling beneath her. "The dalmatian days may be over, but that doesn't mean we don't need some animals around here, all right?"

Chief Johnson rubbed his brow and burrowed the pads of his palms into his eyes. A resounding sigh nearly knocked Krys out of her seat. What was worse? The torrential bullcrap storm she conjured when she helped herself into her boss's office, or that tired face looking back at her? The man was supposed to have a nap at this time of day.

"Kittens," he echoed. "You want the firehouse to adopt a litter of *kittens*."

"Doesn't have to be all of them..." Krys massaged the back of her neck. If her chief was usually napping at two in the afternoon, then she was working out. Lifting weights. Jumping rope. Getting the guys to join her in yoga, because God knew those boys were tighter than the hoses they dragged from engine to hydrants. "Keep a couple so they can play with and keep each other company. I can find homes for the others. I mean, they're good mousers."

The chief propped his chin up on his hand. "So are Dalmatians. You'll notice we never got one. Or a bulldog, for that matter." That was a reference to the poll the weekly town newspaper ran a few years ago. "*What breed of dog do you think befits the Paradise Valley fire hall?*" Somehow, "bulldogs" beat our Dalmatians by over twenty percent. Krys had always thought this a terrier town, so that was news to her.

"If this is about money to feed them and take them to vet, we'll find a way. Remember when they had that library cat a few years back?" Ah, yes, in the days before Yi. Old Smokey and Yi overlapped each other by one year. Rumor was that the cat finally gave up the ghost because it couldn't stand the new head librarian. "They always had a few dollars in the donation bin for food and litter."

"You gonna clean up that litter box every day, Madison?" Chief Johnson laughed as if that were the most ridiculous thing he ever heard. "'Cause I ain't! Doubt you'll find many of the guys here want to pick up cat crap, especially if they already do it at home."

Krys sat back in her seat. "We already share the chores around here. What's cleaning a food bowl and scooping up some clumps?"

"You're out of your mind. Collect some donations for those cats you found, if you want, but I'm drawing the line at inviting them to live here. Do you know how much paperwork that is for me, anyway? Even if I wanted them around..."

Krys knew it was a longshot, but bringing the cats to the firehouse was her best shot at getting all four adopted together. Or at least two of them together. She had already asked her friends if they wanted to adopt some furballs, but Lorri pointed out her upcoming baby, and Jalen admitted she wasn't home enough those days to take care of a pet. The closest Krys's roommate came to helping out was promising to make some fliers to hang around town. *"FREE KITTENS TO GOOD HOME."* Luckily, she had snatched a decent photo of them together the last time she was at Siobhan's place, not that it had helped them get adopted yet.

"If you like them so much, why don't you keep them, Madison?" the chief called after her as she left his office.

"My landlord won't let me!"

"What's up now?" asked Quimby in the lounge. A talk show played on TV. Looked like some serious video gaming had been going on until Tim Young passed out asleep in his chair. "Getting yelled at 'cause you're a girl?"

Krys stopped dead behind the couch. "Who said I was a girl?" she snapped.

It got Quimby every time. He'd be scared witless that he had offended her, only for Krys to slug him in the shoulder and suggest they go spot each other at the bench. *My favorite men are the ones who fall for my dumb jokes.* They were usually the ones teaching her those dumb jokes to use on others later.

"Nah, man." Krys slammed down beside him on the couch. "Was trying to convince him to get the firehouse to adopt the cats."

"You're still going on about those cats, huh? Thought you handed them over to the vet."

"I did, but it's not like the vet can keep them, either. Besides, those furballs need to get fixed before they start inbreeding." That reminded her... "Hey!" She smacked her hand against Quimby's arm. "I'm taking up a collection to pay for their spaying and neutering. You gonna put up twenty bucks?"

"Twenty bucks? Damn. Does that pay for one of them? Do I look like I'm made out of twenties?"

"Pfft. Shoulda known you weren't good for helping out some poor animals that were abandoned behind a barn set on fire."

"Speaking of, did you know the fire marshal still isn't convinced the fire was accidental? He thinks it may have been arson, but I'm not supposed to share that."

"How did you hear that?"

Quimby shrugged. "My girl went to school with his brother. I hear things through the grapevine."

"So it's entirely derivative rumors."

"Derivative? I dunno what you mean."

Oh, my God, Quimby. That high-quality Clark High School education right there. "Basically, you're talking out of your ass."

"Believe it or not," Quimby continued, dutifully ignoring Krys's comments, "those kittens were a big part of him coming to that conclusion. They weren't free roaming after escaping the fire. Somebody put those barn cats in a box and kept them far away from where the blaze would be. You ask me, Longfellow was pulling an insurance scam on an old, crappy building. Thing was a giant fire hazard, anyway. Next wildfire would have knocked it down. Those cats definitely wouldn't have stood a chance then."

"Thanks for the reminder that it's fire season." It had been an awfully quiet one that year. The past two or three years had been nothing but nail-biters by the time July rolled around, thanks to droughts and the drying of every tree in the vicinity. Last year alone, one of the PNW's many wildfires came dangerously close to Paradise Valley's city limits. A few of the rural residents had evacuated into town and were prepared to evacuate elsewhere, too. Like her fellow firefighters, Krys had been ready to join the fight elsewhere in the state, but the city made it clear that they were needed there in Paradise Valley. There were already only three of them who worked full-time. The part-timers and volunteers couldn't make up for them if they were suddenly gone to fight fires elsewhere. Still, it had been rough sitting back and waiting, waiting, *waiting*. Krys had been so paranoid about fires in town that she drove around, looking for illegal burning to report. *They say it's only going to get worse as the years go by. I can believe it.*

Krys shuddered. Quimby ignored it.

"Can't believe Longfellow would burn his own barn down," Krys said, changing the subject. "There's no way he got a decent payout from it. You think it was a controlled burn? No way. You were there. That thing had every opportunity to spread if we didn't get there quickly."

"We got there quickly because Longfellow called us the 'moment he saw it.'"

"Uh huh…" Wouldn't be the first time the firefighters were called in to control an arson burn, but she refused to believe it happened *that* often. "There's still no mama cat, either. Or, at least, I didn't see anything in the debris."

"Could've been a feral cat who thought the barn was a safe enough place to put her kittens. Either way, those kittens are better off at the vet's. Better than being left to the wilds or at the pound. You know what they do to animals there."

"Thanks for the reminder, Quimby! What do you think I'm trying to do, if not get these guys a nice home?"

The snorting of a man rousing from his afternoon slumber startled Krys, who was too uptight for her own good. Tim Young jerked out of his chair, the PS4 controller in his lap clattering to the floor. "When did we get cats? I love cats!"

It took Krys a moment to realize what had happened. In his half-sleep, Young had misheard the incident with the kittens and assumed they were already here, ready to become firehouse cats. The man did love cats, didn't he? He unabashedly carried cat-shaped keychains and had a picture of his own cat as his phone background. His gaming avatars were humanoid cats, and he once told Krys that he used to volunteer at a shelter before dedicating his time to firefighting. If anybody could help her figure out this predicament, it was him.

"I'm trying to get the chief to agree to take the cats in here. Don't you think it's time we got some furry mascots, Young?"

His eyes widened. "I never thought this day would come..."

"He hasn't agreed to it yet. We need to..."

Young leaped up from his chair. It flung back and forth from the impact of his shifting weight, and Quimby was the first to shove his foot against the chair to steady it again. Young stood before them, flexing the fact he was the widest of the full-time crew. It was not all fat.

"How many cats?" he asked.

"Four bouncing baby tabbies."

He looked at Krys as if she might be pulling his leg. "You bring four kittens into this place, and I might die for them."

"Just might?" Quimby quipped. "Whenever you hear there's a cat in a housefire, you're the first one barging through the flaming doors. You're the most popular guy in the calendar because you're always posing with the cats you've saved."

"I'll die for them!"

Clearly, I'm not the one who should be going on a date with Siobhan tomorrow. If Siobhan were straight or Young unmarried,

Matchmaking Madison would be back in business. "So you'll help me convince the chief to adopt them?"

"I got him to use donation money for the new treadmill, didn't I?"

"Thatta boy," Krys said with a grin. "Use those skills of persuasion to save some lives."

At least this was one less thing to worry about. Now, could Krys get confirmation that things would go as well with Dr. O'Connor, the only person in Paradise Valley to look at her and think, *"Yeah, I hate that asshole. Look at her eating her sandwich. Who does she think she is? She probably stole that sandwich from somebody else."*

Krys was a believer in good omens, though, especially when they held degrees of separation from other outcomes she wished to achieve. The kittens were connected to Siobhan. Success with them meant success with her.

Yes, that's how it worked. Krys clung to that belief as she hit their private gym, prepared to be her most toned, fittest self for her date the next day.

Chapter 10

SIOBHAN

This was a mistake. A clear, unbelievable mistake.

I really am an idiot. Siobhan's car crept down Georgia Street, looking for a decent place to park. Cars, pickups, and business rigs clogged the parking lot and street, however. Siobhan didn't think she had to leave a whole hour early to get a decent place to park. Nor did she know of anywhere nearby where she might park without a tow warning. *I should have taken up her offer to pick me up, but nooo, I needed my own escape.* Siobhan still didn't regret driving herself to town. Aunt Gabriella had been insufferable enough finding a suitable outfit and makeup for her niece's "big date."

More like big whoop. Siobhan wore a nice blouse with jeans, but she wasn't about to slap on a dress and makeup. Not for a *movie in the park*. Was Gabriella insane? The evenings may still be warm in August, but temperatures quickly fell once the sun set. Siobhan wore a long-sleeved blouse *and* brought a jacket with her. Besides, a woman never knew when someone like Krys might try to put on the moves. The ol' "oh, you're cold? Here, I'll warm you up!" trick.

I don't think I could stand it. The moment I wonder if this was the same body odor Emily smelled when she cheated on me... Siobhan still wasn't convinced that Krys was innocent. Sure, she might *think* she was innocent. Think being an operative word. *That doesn't mean her hands are clean.* A player didn't keep to only single girls, no matter the intention. Not if given enough opportunity to fool around.

What am I doing? Why am I doing this? Siobhan waited a little too long at a four-way

Hildred Billings

stop. Someone in a tiny green Honda honked at her, propelling Siobhan's car forward as she continued her search for a decent place to park.

She ended up on Idaho Street a few minutes' walk away. After looking around to make sure she blocked nobody's driveway, Siobhan put the car into park and gave herself a pep talk before getting out of the car. *God, I wish I knew more people in town. Now would be a good time to have some friends to fall back on if things blow up with Krys.* Krys had called the office yesterday evening with "big news" to share at their date. About the kittens. *I keep forgetting about them...* Although she didn't usually work with house pets, Siobhan had seen her fair share of cats and kittens. After a while, they blurred together. What made these four so special that everyone bended over backward to change their fates?

Not that she was complaining. The animal lover in her was glad to know they might have care in their near future.

Something stinks, though. Siobhan locked her car and searched for the sidewalk, stuffed with overgrown grass and weeds. Trees in dire need of trimming hung over her head. Rickety fences threatened to keel over. This was apparently not the most affluent part of town. The houses were loved and well-lived in, but at what cost? *This is why I can't stand living in towns. You've got neighbors who don't take care of their properties. Neighbors looking through your window. Neighbors.*

People being people, basically.

"Fancy seeing you again."

Siobhan swerved her head the moment she stopped at the intersection of Idaho and Georgia Streets. Behind her stood a young couple holding hands, probably en-route to the same event. Siobhan didn't recognize the short woman wearing a baggy sweater and running her fingers through thick, auburn hair. She did, however, recognize the taller woman with short hair and a gaze for trouble.

Lorri. From the hardware store.

"Uh, hi." Siobhan forced a grin. "Thanks for the fertilizer recommendation. It's working really well." That was a lie. Kinda. She honestly didn't know how it was working for Aunt Gabriella's garden.

"Oh, good to hear." They continued to wait together as more cars slowly drove by, looking for a place to park. *These two have the right idea, I guess.* Unfortunately for Siobhan, walking was not an option. "You here with somebody?"

"Huh?" Siobhan had not expected such a nosy question. *Right, she's friends with Krys.* Oh, God. Had Krys told her friends she was going out with Siobhan that night? *I'm about to die already.* Siobhan was hoping for a low-key hangout. She wasn't calling it a date anymore. She'd test Krys's behavior, *then* maybe have a date. This was a woman who was cautious in love, after all. "I'm... meeting a friend, yes."

A gap opened in traffic. Lorri stepped forward, her partner's hand firmly ensconced in a strong grip. "Have fun." That was a said with a knowing look.

She totally knows!

Siobhan didn't know where Krys was. Honestly, the more she thought about it, the more she was inclined to turn around and claim to have a stomachache. Didn't help that the park was filled with picnic blankets and towels. A giant screen was erected by the softball area, and the more the sun set, the more Siobhan wondered if she would ever find Krys among the crowd of people out on dates or family outings. Groups of friends smuggled in beer while kids tore up the patches of green between blankets. The occasional man got up to make use of the short line to the men's restroom. The women's, naturally, wrapped around the building. What was worse than a line to the women's restroom? One in Paradise Valley, where a majority of the residents were grown women.

"Hey. Over here."

Krys didn't shout that, yet her voice rammed straight into Siobhan's ear. *How did she do that...* Did her voice naturally carry so well? Was it practice from being a firefighter who had to shout a lot? Or was Siobhan so keenly aware of that voice that she could hear it in the middle of a crowd?

Why in the world was she dwelling on that when she could be taking refuge on a picnic blanket beneath a tree?

Krys had found an ideal spot, although some might not think it was. The tree created a natural wall behind them, and although they were far to the side of the screen, they were close enough to get a decent view. People weren't as likely to bother them since all attention was pointed forward. Yet with nobody behind them, either, Siobhan took heart that she could sit down and not deal with strangers fascinated with her hair. Or the fact she was hanging out with the town player. The fewer eyes on them, the better.

"Sorry I couldn't get us any closer," Krys said. "I had to pick up a shift at work and only got off two hours ago." Her rolling eyes mildly amused Siobhan. Did this mean the best spots were already taken by the time Krys got off work?

The first chill of the evening hit Siobhan as she lowered herself to the blanket. She pulled her jacket closer to her body. Yet she wasn't about to say no to the assortment of cold beverages appearing before her. Sparkling water or soda! Which should she choose?

"I've got..." Krys picked up two bottles of sparkling water, "something called 'Pineapple Passion' and another called 'Berry Blaster.'"

"Pineapple, please."

The bottle was heavy in Siobhan's hand. Or was that how Krys handed it off, as if she didn't know her own strength? *She's the kind of woman you imagine packing you around town. Bam. Right over the shoulder, caveman style.* The crazy thing? Firefighters practiced that move, right? They had to carry people out of burning buildings. They knew all about carrying people.

"Uh..." Krys snapped her fingers to get Siobhan's attention. "Care to share with the class what's got you giggling?"

"I'm not giggling." Siobhan opened the sparkling water and covered her mouth. "You're misreading my body language."

"Suuure." Krys's curiosity remained locked on Siobhan for a little longer than was comfortable. When she finally looked away again, it was with her own smile on her face.

Damnit. She's too good at this. Siobhan couldn't get anything past Krys. Not when the fit and flirty firefighter was aware of every smirk, every laugh, and every flicker of amusement behind Siobhan's eyes. The thought of her knowing what Siobhan was thinking before the woman herself could comprehend the images in her head... yeah, that didn't feel great. Siobhan didn't like it when people read her as easily as they read the Sunday funnies.

"You ever seen this movie before?" Krys asked.

A placeholder image of the movie's DVD cover appeared on the screen. Siobhan shook her head. "It doesn't really seem like my kind of thing. I'm not into absurdist humor."

"Absurdist? Maybe that's what it is. Classic lesbian movie, though. Surprised you've never seen it."

"Do you go out of your way to watch every movie labeled 'lesbian'?"

Krys shrugged. "I guess? Why wouldn't I?"

"Because most of them aren't good…"

"Taste is subjective, huh? You're stuck watching it now. By the end of tonight, we can say you've seen a few things."

Siobhan's breath strangled her throat. *What does that mean?* Krys wasn't under the disillusion that they were getting into bed that night, was she? *I do* not *operate that quickly, even if I'm really into you.* Jury was still out on how Siobhan really felt about Krys. Was she attracted to the abs? Duh. Was she attracted to the attitude and what might lie in their joint history? Absolutely not. Siobhan still wasn't convinced that Krys was innocent. Not in practice. Maybe in heart. *She could be telling the truth while still being guilty.* Siobhan didn't completely see the world in black and white, but when it came to shades of gray, she had to decide which shades were a little too off for her tastes.

"I've got snacks." A knapsack opened. Out spilled an array of crunchy snacks and a pouch of knock-off Twinkies. *Wow. This is high dining right here.* "Sorry it's a weird selection.

Didn't have time to go home or hit the store, so I grabbed stuff from the station. The guys... really aren't healthy eaters."

"It's fine." Siobhan plucked a lunch-size bag of pretzels from the pouch. "I had a light dinner earlier." Gabriella was incensed that her niece *dared* to spoil her appetite for what was sure to be a night of wining and dining with Krys, but Siobhan had a hunch things would pan out like this. A sandwich and some leftover potato salad ensured she wouldn't go hungry, while leaving a little room for a snack.

The lights around the park dimmed. People whistled and kids were recalled to their families. Heads bobbed down. Soon, the only light came from cell phones and the projector.

It was the perfect opportunity for a flirt to "accidentally" wrap her arm around someone. Siobhan braced herself for an awkward hug, as if this were a fifth date instead of a first. Instead, Krys propped herself up against the tree and rubbed her eyes. "If you get cold, there's an extra jacket right there. Ugh. Pray I don't fall asleep."

"Isn't this one of your favorite movies?"

"I've seen it a hundred times before."

What did that mean? Krys easily fell asleep if she had seen a movie too many times before? She could recite it from memory? She didn't want to accidentally spoil something for the virgin eyes in her midst?

Applause echoed in the park as the opening credits began. Siobhan pulled her knees to her chest and wrapped her arms around them. Within the first ten minutes of the movie, she knew for sure that it wasn't her cup of tea, but she would be polite and stay behind until it was over. With any luck, Krys wouldn't fall asleep and leave her there to stew in chilly boredom.

Siobhan glanced at the people around her. A few families had their backs to them, but not too far away was a couple using the darkness as an excuse to make out by the bushes. Siobhan didn't recognize them, especially when it was so dark and she made a point of staying out of town. As long as they didn't start stripping in front of God and Paradise Valley... whatever. Let them play their tonsil hockey.

Halfway through the movie, she realized that Krys had been uncharacteristically silent. Siobhan looked over her shoulder. Sure enough, Krys had folded her hands over her stomach and snoozed against the trunk of the tree. *She fell asleep on our date. Go figure.* Another chill came with the summer night. Siobhan instinctively grabbed the extra jacket on the blanket, assuming it was a spare from the firehouse. It certainly was big enough to fit over her clothes. The hood flipped over her head. Only then did she realize that it smelled awfully familiar.

It smelled like Krys.

What should Siobhan do? Wriggle out of it and brave the cold? Or should she continue to wear it, although it gave her all sorts of twisted... feelings?

This movie really is something else... A bunch of kids sent off to gay rehabilitation camp, played as a dark comedy. Siobhan felt both too old for the humor, but also too young to completely understand where it came from. Her parents were liberal progressives from the city, where Siobhan was exposed to "alternative lifestyles" from an early age. She had her first girlfriend at sixteen, and never looked back. Sure, assholes like Emily tainted her perception of love and devotion, but she never had to lie about who she was or fear for her life.

Maybe that's why I don't really get along with people around here. Siobhan knew that most people moved to this town to get away from their pasts and to raise families in a country setting that wasn't as homophobic as other places. Siobhan had agreed to join Emily here because it had been *her* dream. Siobhan merely appreciated the easy transition into a new career.

What had Krys's life been like before she moved here? Where was she from? Portland? Was there something else about this movie that spoke to her?

Siobhan wasn't going to get an answer anytime soon. Not until the final act began and Krys jerked awake with a few mumbled apologizes. "Geez," she said. "You'd never guess I'm only thirty. Always falling asleep everywhere as soon as the sun goes down. Go figure."

"You have a demanding job," Siobhan said.

"Only when I get a call! We get like... one a day. Maybe. Mostly small stuff."

She didn't say anything about Siobhan wearing her jacket. Not even when the movie ended and they picked up their mess. Both agreed to wait for the others to leave. What was the point of avoiding cars in the dark when they would only be adding to it in a few minutes?

"I actually didn't drive," Krys said. "I only live a few blocks from here, so I walked." She waited for Siobhan to say something. When no words came, Krys continued, "So, uh... you wanna..."

"I better get going." Siobhan turned toward Idaho Street, hoping her car remained unperturbed. "I have a few appointments in the morning and need to sleep."

"On a Sunday?"

Yes. No. Siobhan had no appointments on Sunday morning, outside of emergencies, but she also knew that she couldn't be around Krys for longer than a few more minutes. Siobhan wasn't worried about falling into bed together, but she *was* worried about succumbing to the charms of a master seducer."

"Thanks for inviting me to join you tonight." Siobhan gave a half-hearted wave. "Maybe I'll see you around..."

Was Krys surprised or upset that Krys bailed on her like that? *It's not bailing, though! I stuck around as long as the movie! Bailing would have been leaving as soon as I realized she was asleep, or that I didn't care for the film...* After all, Krys had brought snacks and Pineapple Passion. It was only right that Siobhan be a decent guest.

That's what she told herself as she drove home. Not until she shut off her engine and headed into her house did she realized she was still wearing Krys's spare jacket.

Chapter 11

KRYS

"Hang on, ma'am!" Krys had barely hit the ground before she was expected to jump back up again. "We're gonna get you out of there!"

The adrenaline rush that came with these events never failed to set Krys so far on edge that she could single-handedly upright an overturned car on the side of the highway. Yet that wasn't how it worked. *God knows I wish I could flip this hunk of metal over and get everyone out of there!* That was too dangerous, of course, even if she could physically push that car by herself, let alone with everyone else from the firehouse. Between herself, the chief, Quimby and Young, they had more than enough manpower to move some buildings. Yet they had to wait for the Jaws of Life to make it from the neighboring firehouse in Roundabout, where for some *damned* reason they remained after an incident two months before.

The volunteer crew from Roundabout was skeletal at best, but they were there, and the chief was quick to bark his orders. Every other emergency vehicle in Paradise Valley was also on hand, including the EMTs who waited for the woman currently sobbing upside down in the driver's seat of her totaled car. The sheriff had personally shown up to stand around and give his opinions. Krys would rather have Deputy Greenhill on hand, but apparently it was the day for a county sheriff to strut his stuff in sunglasses and swagger.

Not that she had much time to think about that. Krys was on the frontlines with the Jaws of Life, since she had some of the most training and experience with the unfortunate things.

"Stay still!" Even when victims were male, everyone agreed that Krys was the best to relay information to hysterical people convinced that they were on the brink of death. Maybe they were. Nobody knew for sure until the car was yanked open and the person pulled out. They were lucky that there were no immediate signs of fire. If there were...

Krys didn't want to consider it.

"You got it, Madison?" Chief Johnson called. "On your way!"

She and Quimby were down at the driver's side window, planning the best course of extraction. As soon as the EMTs were given the sign, they brought down a stretcher and their life-saving supplies. The sheriff did nothing beyond stand in front of the local news crew that had been sent to catch everything live on TV. *Great. I always love it when I'm on TV saving a few lives. No damn pressure, right?*

At least this was a good distraction from some of her personal business.

These operations always managed to last an agonizingly long time while also snapping by in a flash. If Krys and Quimby made one wrong move, the woman inside the driver's seat might die. They were lucky if she was conscious. While they proceeded with cutting open the car and calculating how to transfer her to the stretcher, the woman repeated the same prayer over and over, her monotonous voice providing a steady beat for Krys to count by as she backed away with the Jaws of Life and the rest of the crew took over extracting the woman.

She was on the stretcher within thirty more seconds. By then, Krys had taken a deep breath to calm her nerves.

"We'll be staying behind to help with cleanup," Johnson told her a few minutes later. By then, the woman was in the back of the ambulance receiving care. "Good job there, by the way."

"Thanks."

He knew better than to press her for more words. If there was ever a time to be treated like "one of the guys," it was now, when silence said far more than a string of wordy nonsense.

The more busy work, the better. The ambulance tore off into the distance. The worst of it was over. Krys jumped right into whatever needed assistance. The rest of the day would be spent methodically going through the motions to both calm down her nerves and to remind herself that everything would be okay.

"Doesn't ever get any easier," Quimby said on the drive back to the station, "but we did a good job today, if you don't mind me saying so."

Krys snorted. "Yeah, thanks for the help. Couldn't have done it without you."

"Is that sarcasm I detect? Because you *actually* could not have done that without me. It's how physics work."

"No sarcasm." Krys gazed at the passing trees beyond the window. *Let's keep praying that none of them catch fire soon.* There was a close call during a brief electrical storm a few days ago. Sparks had flown when a transformer blew out and some old, dried grass smoldered where it grew. Luckily, the residents who called it in were the same ones who rushed to put it out with buckets before the firefighters arrived. *Those are the people who deserve the medals.* Not that Krys had any medals to give anywhere. She was content with her paycheck, benefits, and occasional dinner put on by the city.

"Hey," Chief Johnson said from the front seat. Young kept the fire engine on steady course back to town. "After we clean ourselves up, I'm ordering us some pizza. My treat."

"Oh, well, if it's *your* treat," Krys said, "then sign me up. I love it when you empty your pockets, Chief."

"You guys keep giving me reasons to spend money on you, and that might happen."

Krys wasn't hungry now, but she knew that as soon as they were back in the safety of the firehouse and cleaned up with showers and fresh clothes, her stomach would gnaw a hole through her skin. The call had come around eleven, a whole half hour before Krys was allowed to take her lunch break. Whatever she had in the fridge to inhale was long forgotten. Pizza sounded *awesome* now that it was well past one and her head hurt.

The best part about being the only woman on the whole squad was that she got to use one of the communal showers all to herself. *She* had no problem with showing off the goods to those she worked with, though. That was all on

Quimby, Young, and Chief Johnson, of course. Too shy for their own goods. Young and Johnson were married, anyway. The chief's wife in particular was a bit weird about Krys being there. *The only reason she doesn't see me as a threat is because I'm gay as hell.* Krys thought about that as she changed into a fresh pair of pants and a PVFD T-shirt she kept in her locker.

The pizza was already ordered by the time she stepped out in her clean change of clothes and wet hair. Quimby dragged her into the lounge, where she watched a recorded replay of the live news footage of their grand rescue. Both Quimby and Madison were on bright display in their gear. Young quipped that this was going to see an uptick in dates for Krys.

"Ladies *love* those Jaws of Life!" he said as he threw himself into his favorite chair. "Every time your hot ass ends up on the news, I swear to God, you've got three dates lined up for a whole week. If I were single, I'd ask you to tell me your magic, but I know where I live. I know what your magic is."

"She's left-handed?" Quimby asked.

"Har, har." Krys was about to say something else, but the ringing buzzer at the front of the station had her leaping out of her couch. "That must be the pizza! TV star's honors, boys!"

She expected to see that Skylar girl delivering the pizza, since she was usually the one who stopped by at that time of day. Instead, an unexpected – but not entirely out of the norm – face popped through the opened garage door by the main engine.

"Since when are you delivering pizzas on the side?" Krys asked the muscular woman carrying a box of delicious carbs and cheese. "EMTs not paying you a living wage anymore?"

That got her a chuckle. Ariana Mura may not have the most chiseled jaw in town, but she knew how to strut. She handed Krys the pizza and said, "Saw Skylar getting out of her car outside and decided to spare her work. Just because you guys are lazy doesn't mean she has to pick up the slack."

"You know her well enough to take pizza from her, huh?"

"You kidding? She's my girlfriend's best friend. We're practically sisters now."

"Well, I ain't tipping you." Krys popped open the pizza box and inhaled. "Now that's the stuff. You know this is our prize for doing our jobs today?"

"Yeah, about that, the whole reason I came by was to tell you that the new girl we've got running with us has got the serious hots for you."

Krys let out a low whistle. She placed the pizza box on the bench nearby and said, "Do I know this lovely young EMT-looker?"

"New girl in town. Name's Sam, of course."

"Because we don't have enough Sams in this butchy town."

"I'm looking at yet another Chris, aren't I?"

"With a *K,* thanks." They didn't mention that most Chrises were actually named Christine or Christina. Krys? Did she really have to say it? *Krystal. That's my name. There. You happy?* She took solace in the fact that women like Ariana were named... that. Made Krystal sound like a perfectly gender-neutral name when someone else shared a name with one of the biggest feminine popstars in the world. *Nobody's looking at this Ariana and mistaking her for overly feminine, though.* "Now, tell me why you're here playing matchmaker for your new coworkers instead of making her have the balls to come over here and tell me herself? She knows I hang at the bar after work, right? I ain't shy." *Not my fault Lorri often looks like she's about to punch somebody. That's her resting asshole face.*

Ariana chuckled. "I was gonna tell her to do that, then I remembered I saw you at the movie the other night with a lovely young lady I hadn't seen around before. So, you know, before I sign her up to get her heart broken by you, thought I'd ask what *that* was about."

"Huh? You mean the redhead?"

"Of course! Mik and I were taking bets that you dragged her here from Portland to show her off, but then you fell asleep."

"How close to us were you?"

"Close enough to see you with someone we hadn't seen before."

Does that mean you and your squeeze were up to no good? Krys had seen the couple slobbering all over each other near the bushes. "Man, everyone in this town is so damn nosy."

"Is it really better back where you're from?"

"Portland? You're lucky if people acknowledge you at all before they run you over with their scooters."

Krys scrambled to think of something to say to Ariana, who wasn't about to budge until she got a few answers about somebody's dating life. Yet before Krys could come up with a convincing story without violating Siobhan's privacy, a head of frizzy red hair appeared in the opened garage door.

"Well." Ariana let out a whistle when she caught the distance. "Guess that answers a few questions." She winked at Krys before turning around again. "Enjoy your pizza. Ma'am." She nodded to Siobhan on her way out. Only then did Krys realize that her jacket was folded over Siobhan's arm.

The sun gave a healthy glow to Siobhan's reddish-orange hair. *I have never seen it that light before. I dig it.* Krys dug a lot of things about Siobhan, though. Like the profile that said she always had a serious thought running through her head. Or the fashion sense of a thirty-something woman who now kept her wardrobe to practical jeans and sweaters. Even now, when it was an easy eighty-five, Siobhan wore a baggy white sweater over a camisole. Didn't look like vet clothes. Had she changed to see Krys?

"If you're here for an autograph," Krys said, hands on her hips, "you're gonna have to get in line. I have a date with some pizza slices before I give myself over to the fans."

Siobhan's hands folded beneath Krys's jacket. "Happened to see you on the news. Pretty cool what you did."

Krys shrugged. "Just another week in Paradise. Could as easily say that your job is cool as hell. Saving those big animals and all."

"Little ones too?"

"I don't wanna step on Dr. Global's toes when his office is a five minutes' walk from here."

Siobhan smiled. Was that one of her genuine grins? The kind that conveyed any and all mirth lurking in her hardened heart? *I must be pretty special if I'm getting those kinds of smiles out of her.* "Seeing you on TV reminded me that I needed to give this back to you." Siobhan held out the jacket. "Didn't realize I was still wearing it until I got home after the movie the other night."

Krys stepped forward and picked the jacket out of Siobhan's hands. "No worries. This is my spare I keep here in my locker for days like today."

Did Siobhan's eyes linger on Krys's chest? *Again?* Thank God she worked out, huh? "Thank you again for inviting me to the movie. It was nice."

"Come on. Admit it. You hated the movie."

Ah! Another smile! "It was fine to watch at least once."

"Speaking of going out..." Krys waited to see if that smile would completely fall. This, after all, a woman who had neglected to contact her since Saturday night. Krys had assumed things weren't going anywhere, although she certainly appreciated the hope that there might be another date soon. "My friend Lorri – you know, the one from the hardware store? – is having a dinner at her place tomorrow night. Turns out I'm gonna be the only one there without a date, because Jalen had to go and bring her girlfriend."

"And...?"

Krys chuckled. "You could be the date of the only woman in town who knows how to use the Jaws of Life. Oh, and Lorri's wife makes some *amazing* food. Like... your tongue will melt out of your mouth and you'll be gone to Heaven. Not to be confused with the café."

Siobhan tilted her head. Was she still thinking about it? Or had she made up her mind long before she came to the firehouse? *I like to think she came here for the sole purpose of talking to me. Yes. I really will play myself up like that.* Only if she could get away with it. Krys often could.

"That might be nice," Siobhan mused. "Neither my aunt nor I are fantastic cooks, but we get by. Haven't had a real homecooked meal in a long while."

"So is that a yes? I don't even have to trot out the celebrity you'll probably get to meet? I mean, she's nice and all, but if you ask me, my friends are way funnier."

"I don't know much about the celebrities, but if you insist…"

"I'm not insisting," Krys said. "I'm asking if you want to come. Oh, and asking for your number, because it's killing me to not be able to text you when I'm thinking about you."

That was the first thing to make Siobhan's face slightly fall. *Great. I pushed it way too far. Good job, Krys.* "Is this thinking happening late at night?" Siobhan asked.

"All hours of the day,"

"Now you're lying."

"Is it really so hard to believe?" Krys picked up the pizza box and opened the lid. "By the way, you should have some of my celebratory pizza."

"First pretzels, now pizza. I really am joining the firehouse diet."

"So is that a *yesss?*"

Siobhan took a slice before turning around and waving goodbye to Krys.

That was totally a yes.

Chapter 12

SIOBHAN

Every time she intended to break things off with Krys for her own damned sanity, Siobhan was sucked back into the whirlwind that was letting her loins do all the talking.

I ate her stupid pizza. Then I went back and said yes to giving her my number. As if Siobhan wouldn't survive if she drove all the way back home and *hadn't given* Krys her number. Besides, that pizza ruined her dinner. Because Aunt Gabriella had grabbed a frozen pizza from her weekly run to Wal-Mart and decided that was dinner that night. *Just wasn't the same as the freshly made stuff from town.* Paradise Pizza didn't make a knock-out pie, but it was at *least* fresh. Papa Murphy's fresh, though? That was debatable…

Now Siobhan was back in town early one weekday evening, staring down Idaho Street as if returning to the scene of a crime.

Wasn't difficult to find Lorri and Joan's house in the middle of the street. Like most of the others, it was a run-of-the-mill starter home, only here in Paradise Valley "starter homes" often lasted one's lifetime. The yards were surrounded with metal fences, and ran the gamut from freshly cut grass and flowers to toys and tools strewn about all summer. Lorri's house was neither a beauty to behold nor a blight on the neighborhood. Yet when Siobhan shut off her car and peeked into one of the front windows, she saw a warm home made warmer with food popping out of the oven.

Someone tapped on her passenger side window.

After nearly losing her lunch to surprise, Siobhan swung her head around and saw Krys standing on the other side of the car. A gesture told her to step out. Since when was she a cop?

"Don't be nervous, all right?" Krys said when she met Siobhan on the sidewalk. "Everyone's really chill. These were the first friends I made when I moved here from Portland, and let me tell you, it was really different from the kind of buddies you make there."

Siobhan had no idea what that meant. She merely followed Krys up the short path and to the Welcome mat.

Krys gave a hearty knock – then helped herself to the door handle.

"Do I smell pot roast?" she called through the crack. "Because you know that's what brought me here!"

Siobhan was soon swept up a flurry of introductions, banter, and pleas to make herself comfortable. She only vaguely recognized a few of the people in the living room. There was Lorri and her partner, of course. Joan was a mousey woman who could barely get a word in edgewise, and this was her own house. She spent more time in the kitchen than she did in the living room, not that there was much room for her in there.

The other couple was less familiar. Siobhan remembered who Jalen Stonehill was after the reminder that she was one of the traveling plumbers in this part of the county. *Right. You've been in my bathroom a few times. Probably my kitchen, too.* Siobhan and Gabriella were handy enough to take care of minor situations, but every once in a while they either had no time or were in over their heads. As for Jalen's girlfriend, the only woman in the room with striking blond hair and a taste of clothing that was decidedly... expensive? Siobhan didn't watch TV much, but she definitely recognized a woman who was used to being on it. Fleur Rosé was a silver screen darling who had stopped traffic when she ran away to Paradise Valley that April. *I had no idea Krys's best friend was the one dating her.* Soon, she would receive another reminder that Jalen and Krys used to date. A really, *really* long time ago. (Those reallys were important, apparently.)

The only one genuinely surprised that Krys brought a date – let alone a date like Siobhan – was Jalen, who only *now* somewhat recognized the vet from the few calls they had made to one another over the years. "She almost never invites anyone to these things," she said with a thicker accent than anyone else in the room. At first, it jarred Siobhan, who was still not terribly used to that rural Oregonian twang that stretched from the coast to the desert. *I'm also not used to it from younger women who look as nice as her...* Who had the twang around there? Farmers with livestock in need of help. Older women who kept close to their lifelong homes. *More proof I don't get out enough.* "How long have you two been going out? I've been outta the loop."

"That's right." Fleur, who had zero accent outside of what one might hear on TV, patted her girlfriend's shoulder before nuzzling a nose into her cheek. It would've been cute, but Siobhan always felt like a terrible peeping tom around people she barely knew. "She's been spending most of her time down in LA. Even this summer, and I don't have to tell you how hot it gets down there during the summer."

"Feels like the devil's blowing fire up my ass," Jalen said with a scratch of her head.

"We haven't been going out for long," Siobhan confessed. "This is our second date."

Jalen's eyes widened. "Really? Wow."

"Should I be concerned?" Siobhan asked.

Krys chose that moment to step out of the kitchen, where she had been giving Lorri and Joan hell for their out of date fire extinguisher. "Bet you guys haven't changed the batteries in your smoke alarms in forever, either," Krys muttered. "I'ma get you a new fire extinguisher, Lor. I can't let you live like this."

"Hey, you think I don't know who to call when my house is burning down?"

"You also know who to call when your dumb ass flips your car over. Although for a true act of dumbassery, I might send one of the guys. Because if you want to see this beautiful, toned ass, you can call me up and buy me a beer."

Jalen laughed. To Siobhan, she said, "Maybe you should be a little worried. Everyone knows how great her ass looks." That garnered a sour look from Fleur. "What? You can see it for yourself! It's right there!"

"What's going on out here?" Krys slammed down beside Siobhan on the loveseat. "You checking out my ass in front of your girlfriend?"

"It ain't like that!"

Siobhan had no idea what to make of this banter. She was knee-deep in old friendships that had been tested to the point nothing could break the bonds. Nothing short of jealousy, perhaps. *Is it really much better to have friendships than romantic relationships? Seems like they end for the same reasons.* People were exhausting. Siobhan almost wished to be back home with her aunt, the woman who yelled at the TV every time her favorite person on some reality show really screwed up... whatever it was they did. Baking. Sewing. Traveling around the world. Snitching on their neighbor for cheating with the mailman...

People were exhausting. The least Siobhan could do, though, was throw herself into suffering through *these* people.

It's not so bad. You should meet new people. Maybe you'll make some friends in this town.

"Chevelle, right?"

She realized Fleur was talking to her. "Siobhan," she said. "The Gaelic name."

"Ooh, I love Gaelic names! You must be Irish, with hair like that!"

And you must be one Nosy Nellie. Siobhan put on a fake smile and said, "My name isn't O'Connor for nothing."

She didn't expect Krys to slam an arm around her shoulders. Yet before Siobhan could ask her what gave her the right, Krys said, "Take it easy on her, would you? She already probably thinks you lot are a bunch of dumbasses."

"Stop projecting how you feel onto her!" Lorri called from the kitchen. "Sorry about that." That quieter voice was a result of Lorri carrying a dish to the table closer to the living room. "Putting up with Krys means putting up with her big mouth."

"You all have big mouths," Joan muttered behind her partner. "Anyway, dinner's ready."

If Siobhan thought that food would shut up a few mouths, she was sorely mistaken. This was small town America, where old friends talked with their mouths open and every other mumbled word was either about college sports or professional athletes in trouble. That was spurred when Jalen made her girlfriend Fleur tell the whole table about an acquaintance of hers in Hollywood. Apparently, some baseball player keen to get into acting and had already botched it by getting caught with steroids.

"The steroids won't cost him a career in acting," Fleur explained, "but his inability to sit on a set long enough to film a few scenes will!"

For some reason, everyone thought that was hilarious. *Are they laughing because she's a celebrity? Because they like her? Or am I missing something about the story?* Siobhan picked at her food, which was perfectly good. At least she hadn't been lied to about that.

"You guys remember those cats I found at the Longfellows' a while back?" Krys said during a small lull in conversation. She soon pointed to Siobhan, currently stuffing her face with noodles. "She's the one I took them to. I showed y'all the pictures I took last time I was over there, right?"

Joan sighed into her glass of water. "I want kittens."

"You've already got one," her partner said, pointing to the growing stomach beneath Joan's clothes. "That's why we can't have any." To the table, Lorri explained, "We ain't getting no pets until the kid's old enough to mind its manners around animals."

"Yeah, yeah, you've told me already." Joan broke off a piece of bread and shoved it into her mouth. *Pregnancy moodiness. See it all the time in animals.* Horses got particularly moody when pregnant. There was one horse owner in the area who had a permanent shiner on his face from that time a horse was tired of him being all up in her business. *You should probably back away, Lorri.*

"It's true that she brought me these little kittens out of nowhere," Siobhan said, speaking up for the first time in a long while. "Imagine my surprise when I came home to find her

standing in my driveway with a basket full of..."
She almost did it. She almost made a crass joke
in front of *strangers*. What was getting into
her? Since when did Siobhan O'Connor, of all
people, sink that low? "Cats."

"Guess she has to be a softie sometimes."
Lorri almost choked on her dinner when she
said that. "Go figure. The woman who wrenches
people out of their cars and puts out the fire in
my kitchen is a big ol' softie."

"Give me a reason to be soft, and I'll be like
that Downy bear from the nineties." Krys
turned to Siobhan. "Remember the Downy
teddy bear? He was always makin' love to those
towels. Really messed me up as a kid."

Siobhan really did not know what to say.

"Screw you, Krys," Jalen said across the
table. "Now I've got that Charmin song stuck in
my head."

"I know the guy who wrote that jingle," Fleur
said.

Every time the conversation started going
one way, somebody had to go and redirect it.
Siobhan could hardly follow what anyone said,

but she knew one thing – they put their hearts and souls into whatever they shouted above the other person. *It's like a dysfunctional family dinner.* When one wasn't showing off a girlfriend, another was chiding someone else for not talking about the giant elephant in the room. Although Joan appreciated it if nobody referred to her as an *elephant,* thank you very much. She said the reason she wore such baggy clothes that summer was because she didn't want people guessing she was pregnant until it was safer to announce it this time around. *"She's had a couple of miscarriages,"* Krys explained at one point. *"They're really cautious about making announcements."* Now it was because she was embarrassed about how much weight she had already put on. Lorri proudly announced that it meant the baby was strong and healthy, obviously.

Siobhan merely wished she hadn't been seated so closely to them. Rather awkward looking at a woman while her partner went on about strong, healthy babies. *You hear it every day in the animal husbandry world... not so much with people.* Siobhan kept her mouth preoccupied with food and drink. Joan couldn't drink any alcohol, but the rest of the table was served with beer and cheap wine. Siobhan limited herself to one small beer since she had to drive later.

In all honesty, the evening wasn't as bad or awkward as Siobhan anticipated. Nobody dug into her personal life once they had the basics in their heads. The cats only came up once more, when Krys told Jalen to "adopt some kitties, for God's sake." *Is she doing this as a show for me?* Or did Krys really care about the animals as much as she portrayed?

It didn't feel like a date as much as it simply felt like hanging out with some people. For that, Siobhan was grateful. Krys's lack of pretenses made relaxing a bit easier, although the "truth" forever tugged at Siobhan's imagination. Was she willing to believe that Krys wasn't a liar? That she really never knew Emily, let alone dated her? Maybe Siobhan could believe that Krys didn't do it on purpose, knowing that Emily was already with someone. But that still left a lot of questions unanswered. Questions Siobhan continued to think about when she knew she needed to let go.

For her own sanity. And her own future.

"Thanks for dealing with those loons tonight," Krys said at the end of Lorri and Joan's path to the sidewalk. Fleur and Jalen had left, and it was *clear* what those two were up to that fine weeknight. Siobhan kept a respectful distance from Krys as they stood beside the car at the curb. "They can be kinda loud and obnoxious. I always forget how much so until I bring somebody new to meet them."

"If they're good enough for a Hollywood starlet," Siobhan opened her car door and remained standing between it and her seat, "then I'm sure they're good enough for me. I'm just not used to a lot of people in general."

"A lot of people?"

"Yes... that was a lot of people. Five strangers for me, anyway."

"*Five?*" Krys leaned against the door. "You're including me in those estimates? Since when am I a stranger, huh?"

"Sorry. Four." Siobhan glanced down the darkened sidewalk. One car with its high beams lit ambled down the residential street. After that momentary blindness, Siobhan asked, "Are you walking home?"

"I usually do."

"It's good exercise, I guess. You don't live too far, do you?"

Krys shrugged. "Over at sixth and Colorado. Not a big deal."

"Still a little ways away..." Siobhan motioned to her car. "You want a ride?"

Although it was dark out, there was enough light from the streetlamps for Siobhan to catch the widening of Krys's eyes. "You're offering me to get in your car and drive me a whole five blocks to my house? A distance that I could easily walk in fewer than ten minutes at a leisurely pace?"

"Fine." Siobhan sat down in her driver's seat. "See you around."

"Whoa, whoa." Krys quickly rounded the front of the car and latched onto the passenger side handle. "Let's not get hasty there, hon. I always accept free rides. I practically do it for a living."

"This isn't a fire truck." Siobhan almost caught herself saying *ain't*. Sheesh. She had been around Krys and her friends too much already. If Siobhan had one thing going for her, it was proper grammar. Most of the time. "I don't have any sirens to set off."

Krys snapped the seatbelt and shut the passenger side door. "Hate to break it to ya, but you already have." She smashed her hand against her chest. "Right here."

Siobhan started the car. "Are you always this cheesy?"

"Only if it's working for you. Otherwise... yeah. I am. Sorry."

"At least you're honest." After a cursory look up and down the street, Siobhan changed gears and pulled out onto Idaho Street.

She needed a few directions in the dark, when it was more difficult to read the road signs. She already had being an out-of-towner working against her, since people who had lived in town for more than a year could walk around the blocks with their eyes closed. Never mind people who were from around there. *I can't imagine growing up here.* Siobhan left that thought in the dust as she turned the corner between Colorado and Arizona. Or was it Colorado and Sixth?

"This is it." Krys was true to her word when she said she lived on the corner. A humble ranch house, like many of the others around it. Siobhan knew that the town was mostly divided by manufactured architecture styles, but it was rather hilarious how quickly things changed from cottage, to ranch, to Victorian-inspired in two blocks. *That's before you hit the trailer park or the two-story craftsmen they built a few years ago.* Emily had wanted to purchase one that had recently hit the market when they moved to town. Siobhan needed the countryside to keep her sanity. "Thanks for dropping me off. Hope you had somewhat of a good time tonight. I kinda worry I keep showing you the most boring sides of myself."

"We both have stressful jobs," Siobhan said, allowing the car to idle. "I figure you're much like me, in that you don't have the patience for more stress in your after hours. I'm all about 'boring' in the evening."

"I mean… hopefully not super boring?"

"Something wrong with dinner and TV?"

"I mean, there's stuff to do *after* the talk shows, right?"

Yes, I get your meaning. Sex. Sex, sex, sex. That's where Krys's mind went, apparently. Siobhan didn't blame her, but it wasn't ideal for a second date conversation.

Or was it?

Pull yourself together. People have sex. You used to like it, remember? Yeah, you and Emily would watch the early viewing of Jay Leno and go to bed earlier. You guys weren't in there to read or catch up on your sleep. Since Emily cheated on her, however, Siobhan's libido had taken a hit. She chalked it up to aging and isolation. The few times she got the urge, she took care of it herself, and often wondered why she bothered afterward.

For every part of her that hated what Krys did to her, there was another part grateful to feel that way again. Yet there wasn't any point to it if it only brought more pain.

"I'm not as big of a prude as you might think I am." Siobhan said.

"Didn't say I thought you were a prude."

"You were thinking it."

"Was I?"

Siobhan cleared her throat. "Maybe on the tenth date."

"You an all or nothing kind of gal?"

"What is that supposed to mean?"

"Uh..." Krys chuckled. "Guess I mean to ask if you're the kind of person who can't kiss without getting busy with it."

Palms sweating and arms stiffening, Siobhan reminded herself to ease up on her grip. "Assumed you were like that."

"You *really* think I can't kiss a gal without inviting her inside for more? Hmph. Maybe you're right, but that doesn't mean I won't survive a little rejection."

"Are you saying that you want to kiss me?"

"You got a problem with..." Krys stopped herself, a laugh breaking through as she looked out the window and toward her darkened house. "Hon, I've been wanting to kiss you since the moment I met you."

That was the cheesiest line yet. Except Krys delivered it with such nonchalance that Siobhan *almost* believed her. *Nobody really means it when they say stuff like that. Such a thing would be ridiculous.* Yet was that a smile peeking on Siobhan's face? Did the girlish side of her want to believe that Krys wanted her that badly? Setting aside the strange truths that might exist between them, it was almost a paradisiacal end to a second date. Krys had a casual stance in the passenger seat that suggested she wasn't going anywhere until she got a kiss.

"You're full of crap," Siobhan said with a grin.

"Yeah?" Krys sat up, but not for long. Soon, her face came closer. The only thing keeping her from kissing Siobhan was decorum. "Try me. Bet it will be the best kiss of your life."

"That's quite the haughty take to have of yourself."

"I'm not saying I'm that good of a kisser, myself. I'm only saying that the right inspiration makes people... better."

"The more you talk, the less inclined I am to kiss you. Ever."

"Yet you haven't kicked me out of your car."

Siobhan had two options. She could either kick Krys out, or she could do something that would make the old her shudder.

She could kiss her. After all, Krys's face was right there. All Siobhan had to do was lean in a little and pucker up.

Do I remember how to kiss? Feels like so long ago...

God, what was she waiting for? What did she have to lose? A little dignity? Ha! She only played at having any dignity. This was a woman who holed herself up in the countryside. Even if rumors disseminated that Krys played her like a sexy fiddle, the public would move on within a few weeks. Considering how things had been going that year, anything could happen to take the spotlight off Krys kissing one inconsequential woman.

Siobhan never envisioned herself as the one who lunged forward for a kiss. Yet that's what happened when she finally gave in to that salty temptation.

Hm. Maybe Krys was right.

Maybe it *was* the best kiss Siobhan ever had. Or, at least, in a long, long while.

There were no expectations harnessed in that kiss. Boom. Lips met. Breaths were caught. A hand touched Siobhan's face as the leather in the seats creaked and eased from Krys leaning closer, closer, *closer,* until Siobhan was pressed against her headrest. Krys offered the kind of power women like Siobhan craved. She didn't want someone to take over in the household, let alone out in public. Except she wanted someone who wasn't afraid to lead behind closed doors. *That same person better be able to sit back and take some of her own medicine, too*. Siobhan couldn't do that on a second date. Maybe not even the tenth. It took her a while to warm up to someone's lovemaking style and figure out how she fit into it. Until then, Siobhan went along for the wild rides coming her way.

Especially since Krys was the kind of kisser who thrived at offering steamy previews of what more may come her lover's way.

"Okay, okay..." Siobhan drew the line at a hand coming for her chest. It was one thing when it was on her face, caressing her cheek and playing with the curls around her ear. Quite another when it went for second base.

"Sorry." Krys sat back a little, but not enough that she was in her seat again. "Got carried away. Good kissing does that to me."

I bet it does. Siobhan put her hands back on the steering wheel. "Glad you thought it was good."

Krys didn't have to ask what Siobhan thought of it. The answer was clear on the grin Siobhan could not contain. "So..." Krys began, a thumb pressing against her window, "I'm pretty sure my roommate is already in a coma for the night. You wanna come in for a bit?"

Siobhan's instincts gave her a resounding *yes*, but that was the thumping of her heart talking. The rational side of her said that once she was in Krys's house so late, everything would end with her clothes on the floor and her face between somebody's legs. *Get it together, Chev. You know your rules.*

"I can't," Siobhan said. "I have to be up early, so I should head home. I'm supposed to be looking at a few sheep." Yeah, that sounded good. Sheep. They needed looking at, sometimes. "Thank you, though."

"Don't wanna keep either of us up too late if we've both got work in the morning." Although Krys was smiling, something in her voice told Siobhan that disappointment hit hard. Krys said she could handle a little rejection. How true was that, though? "Although..."

"Yes?"

"If it's all right, I'll come by tomorrow and pick up those kittens. I've already got a nice place to keep them in garage. My landlord won't ever know. Dude doesn't come up much."

Siobhan sucked her breath. "Sounds good." More like it was an excuse for Krys to come around. "Thanks again for inviting me out."

Krys finally got out of the car. "I'll see you around, Siobhan."

"Chev," she said.

"Hm?"

Siobhan couldn't believe she was doing this. Few were privileged enough to know this name she had since childhood. Who was the last person outside of her family to call her by her nickname? *Emily...* "Chev. That's what everyone calls me." Well, Gabriella called her Chevy, but that didn't need to get around.

"Chev. See you around." Krys shut the door and headed toward her house without looking back.

Siobhan lingered longer than she anticipated.

Chapter 13

KRYS

"I swear to God, if you get us in trouble for those things, I'm kicking your ass from here to Hillsboro." Lucas followed Krys from the kitchen to the garage door, which might as well have been the distance from Paradise Valley to Hillsboro. "What's our lease say? No pets. Come the hell on, those are *pets*."

Krys opened the door. She didn't know what she expected temperature wise, but the blast of warm air told her to get out the air conditioner so the kittens didn't overheat. "They don't count as pets if I'm trying to get them adopted." Phase one of her plan? Wagoning them to the firehouse, where Chief Johnson would *absolutely* fall in love with them and insist on bringing them in permanently. Flawless! Krys wished she had thought of it sooner.

Except she had forgotten a small detail – telling Lucas, her roommate of going on the four years she had lived in Paradise Valley. While they weren't the best of friends, they had a mutual understanding that the house was the landlord's first, theirs second. Probably because they got such a great deal on rent because they were considered "trustworthy." Krys the firefighter and Lucas the maintainer of the church across the street came with glowing recommendations. It meant a nice discount on rent, but that wouldn't last if they mucked it up with a giant mark against their lease.

"They'll be out of here before you know it." Krys shut the door in Lucas's face. Didn't he have better things to do on his Saturday? Like go spruce up the church before Sunday service? The man was a *whizz* with a riding lawnmower and a ladder! There wasn't anything he couldn't do when he got out of Krys's face and did his job across the street!

Krys turned on the light and surveyed the stuffy garage. Right. She needed to grab some kind of portable fan or AC, since it was that wonderful time of year when garages turned into hot boxes if it were only seventy degrees outside.

That day was a little warmer than seventy, though. Augusts were like that, and the kids took every advantage of it as they rushed out on their bikes and scooters. School registration was only a week away. If they didn't have a childhood now, they might miss their chances!

Which means I'll be picking kids out of ditches and off riverbanks this time Monday afternoon... Happened every year. As long as they avoided the forest fires, though, Krys would consider this summer a win.

"Where you guys at?" Krys had hidden the kittens' box in a cooler corner of the garage, but they were more than old enough to jump out and get into a little trouble. The litter box was gently used, though, and the kitten food lapped up like they were growing boys and girls. Before Krys could be too proud, though, she found some kitten puke by a bicycle tire.

She found the culprit sitting on the old, cracked leather seat. He looked at her as if he were the most innocent child in the world.

"Did you eat all the food? Or did you drink too much after you ate?" Krys plucked him up, his little mews of protest and purrs of compliance settling him against her chest. "Who's a pukey boy? Hm?"

She found his brother and one of his sisters, although she quickly realized that the hairy girl was missing. Nothing to panic about. Little Meg loved to crawl beneath drawers and into any bins left half open. Not everything in the garage belonged to either Krys or Lucas, however. Their landlord kept a few *handy* things around. Krys had a few panicked visions of Meg falling into a drawer of nails or getting crushed by an old, rusty rake.

"Meg?" Krys lowered the kittens in her hands and began the hunt for their fluffy sister. "Where are ya, girl? Here, kitty kitty!"

Krys kept a calm countenance, hoping the energy would draw the baby out as opposed to further sending her into hiding. Meg's littermates ran around Krys's feet, as if looking for their buddy. *I've always had the worst luck with fluffy cats. Never had one that lived more than a year.* Now Krys began to panic.

"Meg?" She got down on her knees and looked beneath the bottom of a raised file cabinet. "Where are you, baby? Meg?"

She stopped talking and listened closely. Soon, she heard the pathetic mewling of a kitten crying in the far corner of the room. That... did not sound good.

By the time Krys finally found Meg huddled behind an old bag of fertilizer, she knew something was wrong. The kitten couldn't open one of its eyes, nor could Meg make much effort to come to Krys without breathing so hard that she fell over. This wasn't a cat who had taken a quiet nap away from her rowdy littermates. She was in trouble. If Krys didn't do something, she might lose yet another fluffy cat before it had the chance to turn a few months old.

"You stay there, little girl." Krys grabbed her phone from her back pocket. Luckily, Siobhan had finally given her a personal number to call when Krys picked the kittens up a couple of days ago. "I'm gonna get you help."

The other kittens padded toward their sister, who opened her mouth but didn't make a sound. Soon, she had a pile of gray and black fur surrounding her, her brothers grooming her head while her sister stared at Krys, as if hoping she'd do something.

Anything.

Krys had service in the garage, but for some reason, she couldn't get through to Siobhan. Not without being sent straight to voicemail. *Damnit. Is she out on a call in the middle of nowhere?* Probably. Then again, Siobhan lived on the type of property where a person only had to walk three feet to the left to be in yet another dead zone.

"Hey, Chev." This felt like the wrong time to start calling her that, but Krys only had precious seconds to lose. "One of the kittens isn't looking too great. Can I bring her over? Or maybe you should stop by my place to look her over. I'm not sure if moving her is a good idea."

Siobhan didn't answer for another fifteen minutes. She must have been indisposed.

Shoot. I don't have time to wait for her. Krys looked up the number for Dr. Global's office. At least the receptionist answered within two rings.

Chapter 14

SIOBHAN

Her phone was off. It had been off for two days, since anyone with a medical emergency had a landline to call. A landline her aunt Gabriella could answer and subsequently summon her niece from the darkened dregs of her room.

Not since the days of breaking up with Emily had Siobhan been so sequestered to her bedroom, the curtains drawn and the TV playing the same videos over and over. A woman could only watch an old copy of *Independence Day* so many times, yet the white lines on the screen or the scratchy dialogue didn't deter her from constantly rewinding and replaying it again. Wasn't like Siobhan fully absorbed it every time Will Smith came back on the old analog TV screen. *This is the same TV I had when I moved here with Emily. We bought it from a thrift store when we first got together and had our own tiny apartment. I was in vet school. She was working two part-time jobs so I didn't have to.* That time seemed so long ago now. Another life. A time when a forever together seemed possible. Why would Emily go through all that trouble for Siobhan if she never intended to stay? *If she intended to stray...*

Since kissing Krys the other night, Siobhan had been in this constant cycle of self-beratement. She chastised herself for falling for the playgirl's flirtations. Why, if she insisted on ever dating again, did she have to go for the most dangerous woman in town? Krys may have been interested in her *now,* but it was only a matter of time before Emily Part 2 happened.

Right?

Siobhan couldn't help it. If there was one thing that hurt the most, it was knowing that she had once tasted unconditional love. Maybe that person wasn't the right one for her, but it had *felt* real. Emily had given her such happiness that, even after it was yanked away, Siobhan remained tethered to its chains. *I thought I had moved on...* She really had. A few years should have been more than enough time to get over that heartbreaker. Wasn't that the importance of distance? Maturity? Aging? Aunt Gabriella had been on Siobhan's case for over two years about "getting back on the horse," which was always a strange analogy for a vet who spent some of her days with her arm up a certain animal's rectum. *Anyone who dates me has to be okay with where my hands go...* Emily had often joked about that. Sometimes in front of other people!

That seemed so long ago now. It also felt like yesterday.

No... yesterday... or was it the day before... I acted like a fool in my own car. There had been that part of her desperate to go inside with Krys and make wild love all night long. *The wildest. Like I'm an animal who can't control herself.* Maybe that was the only way Siobhan could stand to do it again. Don't think about anything. Jump right in and pray that she didn't regret it. Rip off the Band-Aid that was celibacy since saying goodbye to the only woman she had ever loved.

I make it sound like Emily really was something special...

Jeff Goldblum made another joke toward his ex-wife. Siobhan slumped across her bed, waiting for the inevitable, sassy comeback. Soon it would switch to a bunch of people on top of the Empire State Building getting blown to smithereens. Then Vivica A. Fox would rescue her dog in the middle of an LA tunnel. Randy Quaid would come out of retirement to save a few lives. Once Jeff and Will were in space, though, Siobhan knew it was time to rewind the tape. She didn't want to be around for the happy ending. She was there for the exploding White House and snappy jokes.

And for Mary McDonnell, one of Siobhan's biggest celebrity crushes. She pretended certain scenes did not happen in the movie.

"Somebody save that little girl," Siobhan muttered about the president's daughter. What was it about '90s movies that envisioned presidents having small children in the White House? *I watched the shit out of that First Kid movie with Sinbad back then.* Did Siobhan have a distinct interest in movies featuring the White House? Why did she enjoy watching it blow up?

Somebody knocked on the bedroom door. Siobhan winced when Aunt Gabriella allowed the hallway light to spill into the dark abode called *sanctuary.*

"Oh, my goodness. You're still doing this?" Gabriella sighed, hand hanging on to the doorknob in case Siobhan got any ideas about closing it again. "When are you going to finish whatever the hell this is? Don't you have appointments to get to? Cows to save?"

"I haven't gotten any calls," Siobhan muttered. "I've honored my appointments. There ain't no cows dying out there?"

"You sure about that? Because I just got off the phone with somebody."

All right, that would get Siobhan off her bed, but not to indulge conversation about her personal life. If a cow needed saving, she supposed she could get off her ass and back to work. At least it took her mind off other things. Like how much her heart hurt every time she saw another couple reunited in that stupid movie.

"What happened?" Siobhan asked. "Who is it? Is it an emergency?"

Gabriella was not quick to answer. *What? Seriously. What's going on? If something or somebody's in trouble, I better be told sooner rather than later. Is time of the essence?*

"Krys called me a few minutes ago." Gabriella cocked her hand on her hip. "Said you weren't answering your phone."

"Come on, now!" Siobhan sat back down on the edge of her bed. "That doesn't count! I thought this was a real animal emergency."

"It could have been, since the reason she was calling you is because one of those kittens got sick and she was worried half to death about it!"

"What? What's wrong with it?"

"Hell if I know. She said she got it in to see Dr. Global since you weren't answering."

"For the best, then." Siobhan sighed. "If she's in town, it's much faster for her to take it to Dr. Global. Might not be much I could do to help it."

"That's not the point, Chevy." Gabriella sighed. "I thought you were sweet with her! Weren't you two going out?"

"We had a couple of dates. That doesn't mean it's going anywhere."

"For God's sake, Chevy, it's like you don't know how dating works. I'd never guess you were in a relationship before."

Siobhan slammed a pillow over her head. "Get off my ass about it!"

She should have known Gabriella would march over and rip the pillow off her niece's face. "I know one thing for sure, hon, and that's you shouldn't string a nice young lady along like she's your puppet. If you're not going to call Krys back about the cat, the least you could do is call her and tell her you're done talking to her. That way she won't keep calling the landline like some lost little puppy that only wants your attention."

Lost little puppy? That didn't sound like Krys at all. That sounded like Siobhan, who wandered through her own personal life like a dog let off its leash. She had enjoyed the freedom at first, of course, but once she realized she was disconnected from her home, her family, she looked around in fear and wonderment. Where was she supposed to go? How would she get home? Was there a chance at starting over again, assuming she survived these trying times?

Or would she be caught by the dog catcher and sent away for good?

"Bah." Gabriella washed her hands of it. "I can't deal with you right now. I have to go into town and get us some food. Somebody's been eating through our stash of chips. Like they're her *meal* or something."

"Don't get the really expensive ones, okay?" Siobhan meekly called after her. "No sense wasting money on the name brand when the store brand does a good enough job."

A grunt told her that her aunt was leaving.

Siobhan didn't bother rewinding the tape of her favorite movie. She got up and headed across the hall to use the bathroom. While in there, she decided that it was high time to take a shower and get some of the blubbery sweat off her body. By the time she stepped out, fresh and clean from her shower of woe, she realized that somebody was downstairs.

It did not sound like Gabriella's footsteps.

Indeed, her car was not in the driveway when Siobhan glanced out the bathroom window. She saw another car instead.

A familiar car that did not belong to either her or Aunt Gabriella.

"What the hell?" Siobhan fluffed out her hair and made sure her thin bathrobe was tightly tied before stepping out of the room. The footsteps continued to pound on the floor beneath hers. By the time she reached the bottom of the stairs, everything she feared had come to light.

Krys stood outside the front door. She hadn't helped herself inside, although odds were strong that Aunt Gabriella hadn't bothered to lock the door when she left. Simply put? Krys's footsteps were so heavy in those boots of hers that they practically smashed through the fragile porch wood.

She didn't say anything. Nor did she pound on the screen door. She merely paced back and forth, as if trying to think of what she would say when she finally called Siobhan down from her tower.

Siobhan would catch her unawares. That was the only upper hand she had as she swung open the door and asked, "What are you doing here?"

Krys hadn't been prepared for Siobhan's presence. She was less prepared for nothing more than a bathrobe.

To be fair, that hadn't been part of Siobhan's plan, but she was committed now, wasn't she?

Your final test is to see if you can keep your eyes on mine, Madison. For someone like Krys, that could be the hardest challenge of her life.

Chapter 15

KRYS

There were half a dozen things Krys anticipated when Siobhan finally showed her face. A bathrobe thin enough to show off some of the goods was *not* one of those things.

Holy hell... Was this a joke? Krys came down here to make a case for living creatures, which may or may not have included herself. *Not to instantly forget everything I was about to say because I suddenly have a hot woman in front of me.* Siobhan was always hot, yes, but never before had Krys seen her wearing so sexy. This was a woman who wore jeans and sweaters. Maybe a light jacket, if she were feeling frisky.

Her lab coat did plenty for propriety. What would Krys learn next, though? That the woman she had fancied since first seeing her *didn't* sleep in footie pajamas or baggy T-shirts? Did she sleep in cute, silky negligees, too? Or, *gasp,* in the nude?

Get a hold of yourself! That wasn't a flirtatious look on Siobhan's face. If Krys wanted to accomplish anything, she better keep her eyes off those nipples and on Siobhan's ticked countenance.

"Why aren't you answering your phone?"

Ah, yes. Utterly accusatory. Way to go.

Siobhan barricaded the door with her body, arm slinking up the frame and ankles crossing. Those bare toes dug into the vinyl flooring beneath her feet, but Siobhan didn't seem to care if it was clean or dirty. She only had eyes for Krys. Angry, dagger-like eyes that were not in the mood for her crap.

"I didn't realize I owed you any time on the phone." Siobhan said.

"You got a problem with me?" Krys knew how to be intimidating... to the point that she was keenly aware of her body language when she took a small step forward and loomed above the woman before her. She didn't want to intimidate Siobhan. This wasn't a shake down or promises of retribution if she didn't get her way. Yet that didn't mean Krys would back down before the woman who thought she could play obnoxious games.

"I have problems with people who don't know how to stay away for five freakin' minutes. Ever heard of personal space?"

"There's asking for personal space, and there's refusing to answer calls so soon after a first kiss. You know what kind of message that sends someone? Hm?"

Siobhan tilted her head. "Why are you so obsessed with me?"

"Obsessed? Don't flatter yourself. You make me sound like I can't control myself. I'd beg to differ." Krys scoffed. "I like to think we're going out. Maybe you're not my girlfriend, but I'm at least owed the courtesy of an explanation."

Siobhan almost said something. Instead, she lowered her arms and looked away. Her countenance softened. Barely. "I haven't been feeling well." She looked back at Krys. "Sorry I haven't been answering my phone outside of veterinary emergencies."

"I had one earlier, actually. Remember Meg? She got sick, and when I tried calling you, I kept going to your voicemail."

"My aunt said you called. I'm sorry I couldn't help, but you did the right thing taking her to Dr. Global instead of me. There's only so much I can do for small animals way out here. If you have a cat and you live in town, you should definitely take it to the clinic."

Krys could hardly believe it. Siobhan was so nonchalant about it! Didn't she understand what had almost happened? *The kitten will be fine, Dr. Global said, but only because I found her in time. The poor thing was so dehydrated they're keeping her at the clinic overnight, and now I have to figure out how to get the kittens inside the house.* Because Lucas would love that. He could suck rocks, though. Krys wasn't about to let any of those kittens die on her watch, especially because of her own stupidity.

I knew the garage was too hot, but I thought I could make it habitable in time... She'd have to keep them in her room, huh? Well, at least she could keep it cool. This only compelled her to get those cats moved into the firehouse faster.

"You think this is only about the cats?" Krys shook her head. "I don't know how many times I have to tell you that I never dated your ex. I'm sorry that she cheated on you all over town, but that's not my problem. Nor is it my responsibility, even if I *had* accidentally dated her. You ask me? You're scared of being in any relationship, let alone with me."

Siobhan fired up some derision so quickly that Krys worried she might have to call the volunteers working at the firehouse that weekend. "What the hell do you know about me? It's none of your business how I feel about one thing or another. You think I *need* a relationship to be happy? Maybe I don't look like I'm living the life, but I was perfectly content before you came blazing through here and dragging up bad memories left and right."

"Why content when you have happiness?"

Siobhan stepped back with a wrinkle of her nose. "Do you think you're so cool because you get any woman you want in town? Because that doesn't impress me. Maybe I don't want to date somebody who gets off so much on it."

"I don't *get off* on having an active dating life, thank you very much. In fact, I'll have you know that I hadn't been dating anyone almost the whole damn year before I asked you out."

"Again, is that supposed to impress me?"

"You know what?" Krys smacked her hands against her legs. "This isn't about me. Last I checked, I was asking *you* what *your* problem is."

"You wanna know my problem? *You're* my problem!"

That was the first time Siobhan raised her voice to Krys, who had been expecting yet another muted response. "Okay, then." She turned, but not to walk away. Not yet. Perhaps a woman merely needed to process that first. "Am I your problem because you hate everything you think I stand for? Or because I'm making you think about unpleasant things?"

Siobhan opened her mouth. Nothing came out. Nothing but a huge breath that sounded more tired than the bags beneath her eyes looked.

"Who said those things don't go together?"

Krys gritted her teeth. "Can I come in, at least? Just tell me what's on your mind. I can't be expected to get to know you better if you're always pushing me away."

"Maybe you should take the hint! Because you know what? I don't owe you anything. I shouldn't have gone on those dates with you. I don't know what I was thinking kissing you."

"Why did you have to be thinking anything? Why can't you let go and enjoy something for once?"

"What makes you think I don't enjoy anything?"

"I know you enjoyed that kissing the other night."

Sometimes, Krys was too simple for her own good. When she said something like that, she often got a chuckle or a sagely nod out of someone. Not from Siobhan, who looked at her with aghast disbelief. Two seconds later? She craned her head around and covered her eyes before a sob broke free.

Krys had two sturdy shoulders to cry on. A woman only had to choose which one she liked more. The left one? Perfectly suited for feeling the thumping of her heart as it did its best to console everyone within a few inch radius.

Siobhan probably didn't want to come anywhere near Krys, let alone touch her. Yet she didn't put up a fight as Krys passed through the screen door and wrapped her arms around one person in so much pain. Siobhan buried her face against that left shoulder and unleashed two more large sobs that soon wettened the T-shirt clinging to Krys's torso. *She feels so frail in my arms.* She hadn't the other night. Siobhan had felt perfectly strong for someone who had lived thirty years on Earth and had already seen her fair share of crap.

"You need to cry?" Krys said. "You go ahead and cry. No need to keep all that shit inside."

Siobhan clung to Krys's shoulders. Slowly, she lifted her head. Somehow, she wasn't as puffy or red as Krys anticipated. Yet her bottom lip did shake, and before Krys knew it, someone hugged her with all the strength in one's body.

"I'm sorry," Siobhan said through deepening sobs. "I don't know why I'm still so hung up on it. I guess... seeing you around so much lately reminds me of everything that happened between... everyone."

"It's not everyone." Krys didn't know how she got that out so calmly, God knew she wanted nothing else but to shake Siobhan by the shoulders and try to rattle some sense into her head. Yet Siobhan didn't need that. What she needed was some kindness. Some tenderness. Someone who could prove, once and for all, that there was real love to be had out there. "It's you. *You* and that spineless, cheatin' ex you had. I'm sorry, hon. Nobody should have to go through that. I wish I could wipe that all away for you, but I can't. So you'll have to trust me. So help me God, if I turn out to be another untrustworthy person in your life, that's all on me. Not you. It says *nothing* about you."

Had she finally pressed upon the real issue plaguing poor Siobhan's heart? *It's never been about me. It's always been about her and the pain she feels when she looks at someone like me.* Krys had seen pictures of Emily, mostly to confirm that, no, she had never dated that person, either unwittingly or not. They didn't look that much alike, but maybe they had similar personalities. Was that what Siobhan saw when she hung out with Krys? A personality that made her ill?

"All I ask for is a chance." When Krys pulled back and looked down again, she met the hopeful face of a woman in pain. How long had Siobhan held this inside of her? How much did she repress to keep her sanity over the years? She had never properly expunged it, had she? *She's so tough. She's tougher than me. She's too tough for her own good.* How could a woman be expected to heal and move on if she kept those feelings inside of her, never to properly deal with them until it was too late?

Siobhan stepped back and wiped the tears. "I don't have a lot of chances left to give."

"I'm not saying we're gonna be together forever, Chev. We're still getting to know each other. Maybe we've got something here. Maybe we're gonna fizzle out by the end of the year. How are we gonna know if we don't try, though? Would you rather part ways now and never try? Or do you want to prove to yourself that you've got what it takes to move on from that asshole who broke your heart?"

Siobhan's eyes darted back and forth, as if she searched for the answer written somewhere on Krys's T-shirt. "You're right. Of course you're right. I don't... I don't want to live the rest of my life wondering what the hell I'm waiting for. It's been a few years, yeah? Maybe it's time to address what's left in my heart and move the hell on."

"You don't have to do it alone."

"I don't know why you're so insistent about being around me, Madison." Krys had already gotten used to the way Siobhan said that name. Sounded *nothing* like the way the crew at work said it, yet somehow she retained the same sarcastic bite every time she looked Krys in the eye and called her by her last name. *Doesn't matter if her eyes are puffy and red. She's got that bite.* Krys always knew she needed a woman with a little teeth on her. It was the only way to keep her in line!

"I admit, I was first taken in by your exponential beauty." Whew. There was Krys's three-dollar word for the day. *Watch out. I might come out looking too educated for this town. Maybe not educated enough for a doctor, though.* "Then you opened your mouth and only made me want you more."

"God knows why."

"Do you need an explanation? Sometimes you gotta let nature take its course, girl."

"I hear you do a lot of that."

Siobhan was back to her biting commentary, but it was better than the tears and denials of their mutual attraction. She could be as snarky as she wanted if she kept up that smile and batting eyelashes that brought Krys back into a light and loving embrace.

"I'm a fan of going with the flow, yeah, but it's not only my flow I've gotta heed. When someone else is in the picture, we've got our own mutual flow, yeah?"

With her head cocked to one side, Siobhan asked, "Do you want to shut up and come upstairs with me?"

Hello. Moving quite quickly all of a sudden, aren't we? Krys was game, but she also knew that Siobhan was in a fragile, emotional state. Hormones could be set aside to make sense of emotions, yes? "I wanna come upstairs, yeah," Krys said with a bite of her own. "But I don't feel like shutting up. Got too many flows to talk about."

"I can't tell if you're making me think about yoga or my period."

"*Your* period? Pfft. Was talking about mine."

Siobhan's hand lingered in Krys's as she turned around and slowly walked to the staircase. "Get the hell upstairs, would you?"

Her intent was impossible to read after that flurry of emotions. Yet Krys knew that, as long as she kept her cool, she could navigate anything heading her way. Even a woman who might be acting a little too quickly.

Yet Siobhan didn't have carnal intent on the mind. As soon as they were in her room and the door softly clicked behind them, Siobhan crawled onto her mussed bed and gestured for Krys to join her.

This wasn't how Krys planned on spooning her new girlfriend for the first time, but she wasn't opposed to it. Siobhan was so soft in her thin bathrobe that it was as good as making love. One arm over her. Nose in her mess of hair and searching for the back of her neck. Krys almost forgot to take off her shoes before climbing onto the bed. She also tried not to think about the fact that this was probably the bed Siobhan once shared with Emily – and that Krys was probably the first lover to lie in it since.

"I guess it isn't so bad letting go sometimes," Siobhan whispered.

"Yeah, only do it sometimes. Otherwise you might enjoy life a little too much."

That inspired Siobhan to turn over, her lips close enough to kiss. Somehow, Krys refrained. "You're infuriating."

"You're the one who invited me into your bed."

"You saying I only have myself to blame?"

"No, ma'am," Krys said with a snort. "I'm saying that you can't blame *me* if I hold onto a little hope here. You're so cool it almost tears me up inside. I keep thinking about how much I've gotta kiss you."

"You've *gotta?*"

"I've gotta, yeah."

Siobhan came dangerously close to making that a reality. Not until she reopened her eyes and gave Krys a pout did her lover realize that a kiss was, indeed, beseeched.

There's a five-dollar word right there... Krys was quite smug as she leaned in for that kiss.

They didn't stop with one simple kiss. It wasn't that kind of day.

Chapter 16

SIOBHAN

One of the signs hanging in the darkened windows was half blown out. The yellow sign advertising a popular local IPA couldn't quite get all its words out anymore. The half that had blown out took out the important letters in CASCADE LOCKS and made it look like something completely different and tongue in cheek.

Yet another sign that Siobhan should probably not go inside. This wasn't a place for her. She was too delicate, too sensitive to handle the kind of rowdy crowd that hung out at a dive bar on Friday night. Siobhan took a deep breath and turned around, prepared to return to her car and text Krys that she couldn't make it.

She had withdrawn her phone from her back pocket when something else replaced it. Namely, a hand lightly tapping her ass.

"Hello, gorgeous." Krys wrapped her arm around Siobhan before she had the chance to round on her assailant and give them what for. *Just because I let you smack my butt in the privacy of your bedroom doesn't mean you can smack my butt in a dimly lit parking lot!* Yet how could Siobhan stay miffed at the woman nuzzling her cheek and calling her gorgeous? "You ready to go in? It's wings night. Let me tell you, they ain't too bad."

"I... I thought you would already be in there."

"Nope. Running a bit late because we had a call late this afternoon and I needed a damn shower. Some punk burned down another barn a few miles out of town."

"That's terrible!" Did that mean that the fire marshal's suspicions of arson at the Longfellows' farm were true? Did Paradise

Valley have a fire bug on the loose? "But did you find a basket of bunnies or puppies this time?"

"Hon, if I had found such a thing, you'd be the first to know. As always."

Krys kept her arm wrapped around Siobhan's shoulder as they approached the bar. Tom Petty blasted from the speakers. *The only thing I know about him is that he played on* King of the Hill. *I think. Was that him, or Huey Lewis? Oh, God, I don't know which is which.* Would this be on a test later? Was karaoke expected at the lesbian dive bar? *Straight people karaoke all the time... I can only imagine...*

What did it mean if her extent of '80s music knowledge was focused on Tiffany, Heart, and not much else? Did knowing one song from the Bangles and Pat Benatar help?

"You look like there's a ghost standing in the doorway." Krys lowered her arm to open the door for Siobhan to step through. "Come on, Chev, it's a bar, not a ritzy ballroom."

I think I'd feel more at home in a ballroom... "I really don't know much about these places."

"What's there to know?" Siobhan barely heard Krys over the blast of music, clacks of the pool tables, and rabble of voices coming from both the bar and the booths in the back. For every couple on a date, there was a small group of friends shooting the shit or challenging old, bitter rivals to a round of pool. *Not a karaoke machine in sight...* The strangest thing, of course, was the presence of men. A whole group of them sat in a corner booth. Construction, from the looks of it. 'Twas the season of road and roof repairs, but Siobhan never expected to see them in a lesbian bar. Yet nobody paid them any mind, and the waitress bringing them wings and beer went as far as to shove her tray against her hip and brag that her favorite football team was gonna whoop theirs that upcoming season.

I don't understand anything... Siobhan kept her head craned around as Krys led her to the bar. Because heaven forbid they grab a booth and be allowed to hear each other.

If she thought she was about to be saved, she could have another think. Because once Lorri and Jalen caught sight of her, they waved them down and asked if they should move to a booth. Krys was the one who insisted they stay at the bar because, according to her, it was easier to hear everyone there.

Her friends may have found it strange that Krys and Siobhan were still dating, but they didn't say anything. Nothing besides greetings, polite questions about her work and her aunt's health, and that she was a pretty sight for sore eyes. Siobhan was certainly more "country" than the other partners at the bar, but that didn't say much. When Jalen dated a literal Hollywood starlet and Lorri was attached to Paradise Valley's own Susie Homemaker, all Siobhan had to do was put on a pair of sturdy boots to get called semi-butch. *I know they're joking, but it's so weird they talk about these things... let alone right in front of me.* Would Siobhan ever get used to it?

Right. She was here for Krys, who made it one of her missions to include Siobhan in everything. Sometimes, like tonight, she agreed. This was part of her self-improvement to go into town more often and socialize with people who weren't named Gabriella O'Connor. Aunt Gabby loved it, of course. When Siobhan announced she was going out with Krys to the bar that night, Gabriella practically handed her a jacket and a condom. *I don't think she knows how this works...*

The best thing everyone could do was not completely ignore her while also foregoing any forced interactions. Siobhan had a soft drink alongside her wings while Krys pounded back a beer and her friends drank more. *Suspicions say she drinks more than that... when I'm not around.* Did this mean Krys was putting on sober airs for her the new girlfriend? Or that she wanted to stay sober for the end of their date?

When would the date end? When they left the bar? Or would Siobhan once again find herself in front of Krys's house, kissing her while fighting the temptation to head inside? *Again?*

Krys did have a nice, comfortable bed. Siobhan sank into it so easily that she turned into a true pillow princess for the first time since she could remember. She also embarrassed herself around Krys's roommate, Lucas, when she stepped out to use the bathroom the next morning wearing nothing but one of Krys's T-shirts. She had totally forgotten that Krys lived with anyone, let alone a guy!

But, if that were the most embarrassing thing to happen so far, she must not be doing too poorly. Their short relationship had already survived an emergency call for Krys during one date and one for Siobhan in the middle of a sleepover. Whether a car was overturned on the highway or a barnyard animal had fought off a cougar, they were well versed in the meaning of, "*Sorry, got a call. Have to go.*"

So far, it hadn't presented too much of a problem. Krys said it helped that there were no wildfires. Yet. They still had to survive September.

"You know what?" Lorri pointed to Krys after they finished their dinners. "I think this is the first time the three of us have all had steady partners at the same time. I mean, you guys have been catching up to me for however many years, buuuuuut..."

"Oh, get over yourself, Lor." Krys laughed. "We've always been dating. To some extent." She cleared her throat for Siobhan's benefit.

"Maybe you have, but Jay was the unluckiest person at getting more than one date with someone until that actress came along. That was around the time you had stopped dating altogether, so it was like the universe had spun on its head and no longer made any sense. To my humble, coupled ass, anyway."

"Do you hear this?" Krys said to her girlfriend. "She thinks she's Captain Domestic."

"Ten years from now, when we're all sitting here with our kids, you're still gonna give me crap, Krys?"

"If in ten years you're hauling your kids into a *bar,* I'm personally calling the deputy the haul your ass back into that cell you love so much."

"I oughta wring your..."

Siobhan immediately went onto the defensive, but Jalen didn't look too bothered by the altercation erupting between them. She continued to drink her beer before calling over Lorri and Krys's heads, "So, how are those wings? Good, huh?"

Siobhan couldn't help but laugh. Three seconds later, Lorri and Krys were still best friends, and everyone wanted to hear about how the kittens were doing.

If this were another night living and loving in Paradise Valley... well, Siobhan supposed she could get used to it. Sure beat locking herself up in her house for the rest of eternity and having nothing to do with anyone besides her aunt and a few select animals she was paid to treat.

The fact that she had been in this bar this long and only *now* started to think about Emily... well, perhaps that was progress.

Siobhan would take it.

Chapter 17

KRYS

"Welcome to your new home, buddies." Krys hoisted the kitten carrier between both hands, body swaying to the beat of their insistent mewls. "Look at all the space you have to run around and be little assholes. Ain't it grand?"

No one was more excited than Young, who had personally assisted Krys with bringing the cats over on their lunch break. The plan hadn't been to press the issue until after the kittens were fixed and recovered, but Lucas received a call from their landlord two days ago saying a "visit" was on the horizon. The cats had to get out. Now.

Johnson was the man to give the all clear for these little bundles of furry joy joining the team indefinitely.

"Oh, oh, let them out over here." Young rushed to the lounge, where he had built a respectable cat tree made of recycled materials from the county dump. Johnson had donated an old blanket as good faith to the kittens. Quimby bought a cat toy and dangled it from the top of the tree. Krys made sure it was positioned fairly between the big windows and the human furniture. Slowly, but surely, parts of the firehouse would be adequately transformed into a living and playing space for four rambunctious kittens who were sure to turn into lazy, lazy adults one day. God knew they got plenty of sunlight in there, even during the winter.

One by one, kittens sprang out of the carrier. It made for grand introductions.

"That one's Beckham." Krys scratched the little guy leading the charge, his tail of curiosity erected and his nose sniffing the air. "This one's Pelé." His brother with the dark M on his forehead joined him at the edge of the couch. Grooming would be necessary to keep them from scratching it.

"I'm sensing a pattern here," Quimby said behind them.

"And this is Mia..." The short-haired girl went off in another direction, forging her own kitten-led path. "And this is Meg." The little shy fluffy girl needed some help out of the carrier. Once she was out, though, she trotted right over to Young, who was in tears already.

"Mia, I get," Quimby said. "But Meg?"

Krys shot him a critical look. "Megan Rapinoe. Hellloooo."

"Got it. Soccer people." He chuckled. "You know I ain't much into futbol."

"One of these days I'm dragging you to Portland and making you watch a Thorns game."

"You lost me at *Portland*."

Johnson came out of his office to see what the commotion was about. "I see the gang's all here. Now, remember what I said about taking care of them? I'm not cleaning *any* litter boxes."

"I would consider it an honor to clean their litter boxes," Young said.

"You are a weird, weird man, Young." Johnson shook his head. "Bless you, though."

A shadow appeared in the opened garage door. One glance over her shoulder told Krys that her favorite person had stopped by, because that was absolutely Siobhan's work truck parked along Main Street.

And that was *definitely* Siobhan standing in the doorway.

"I didn't know today was D-Day." Arms akimbo, Siobhan patiently waited for Krys to come over and give her a kiss. The boys pretended they hadn't noticed. Besides, Young was chasing kittens and Quimby decided now was the time to readjust the cat tree. Again. "I see everything is under control."

"Think I don't got this?" Krys might have flexed when she said that. "Kittens? Piece of cake now. They'll totally be..."

"Damnit, it's chasing my shoelace!" Chief Johnson cried.

Krys flinched. "It's fine. Like you, yeah?"

"I can't tell if you're asking me how I'm doing, or asserting my appearance, as you usually do."

"That one, but I also don't mind you telling me how you're doing."

Siobhan didn't get a chance to say. The moment she opened her mouth, the fire bell went off, and nobody – least of all Krys – could get a word in edgewise over the commands of the Chief.

"Looks like another barn fire off the highway! Come on! Let's go! Look alive, Madison!"

"Apparently, I've gotta go." That was said in between bursts of concerns about the cats and Quimby struggling to get into his clothes. "Good thing I had lunch, huh? I hate it when these calls come in right before or, God forbid, *during* my lunch break!"

"From what I've noticed around here," Siobhan said as her girlfriend came closer for a hello/goodbye kiss, "anytime you're not fighting fires, you're on lunch."

"All in a hard day's work. Where you off to?"

"Just got back from shoving my hand in places you don't wanna know about."

"Madison!" Johnson shouted. "Stop flirting with your lady and let's get going!"

Krys stole that kiss as she turned around and shot for her locker. Siobhan was still on the sidewalk by the time the fire engine, sirens wailing, pulled onto Main Street and made its way toward the fire.

Now there's a sight... Krys leaned out the window and blew a kiss to the woman waving back at her. Two seconds later, little Megan Rapinoe bobbed out of the opened window and made her great, grand escape into the depths of Paradise Valley.

Siobhan took off after her. *Eh, they'll be fine...* Krys had a feeling this was only the beginning of the fun they'd have – with or without animals getting between them.

Or bringing them together, really.

Hildred Billings

Hildred Billings is a Japanese and Religious Studies graduate who has spent her entire life knowing she would write for a living someday. She has lived in Japan a total of three times in three different locations, from the heights of the Japanese alps to the hectic Tokyo suburbs, with a life in Shikoku somewhere in there too. When she's not writing, however, she spends most of her time talking about Asian pop music, cats, and bad 80's fantasy movies with anyone who will listen...or not.

Her writing centers around themes of redemption, sexuality, and death, sometimes all at once. Although she enjoys writing in the genre of fantasy the most, she strives to show as much reality as possible through her characters and situations, since she's a furious realist herself.

Currently, Hildred lives in Oregon with her girlfriend, with dreams of maybe having a cat around someday.

Connect with Hildred on any of the following:

Website: http://www.hildred-billings.com
Twitter: http://twitter.com/hildred
Facebook: http://facebook.com/authorhildredbillings
Tumblr: http://tumblr.com/hildred

Made in the USA
Columbia, SC
26 July 2023